THAT SHAKESPEARE KID

By Michael LoMonico

ISBN: 1489598227
ISBN 13: 9781489598226
Library of Congress Control Number: 2013912287
CreateSpace Independent Publishing Platform
North Charleston, South Carolina

To Michael and Jake and all students of Shakespeare:
Speak his words, see his plays, and learn to love him.

"To the great Variety of Readers. From the most able, to him that can but spell: There you are number'd."

These words appear on one of the front pages of a book we call the First Folio. It's a collection of Shakespeare's thirty-six plays published in 1623, seven years after his death. John Heminge and Henry Condell, two friends of Shakespeare, wrote an introduction for the First Folio to let the world know the book was for all people, not just the rich and famous.

While I can't say this book you are about to read is even remotely as important as the First Folio, I'd like to think it was also written for that "great variety of readers," not just the smart kids in the honors classes.

I've taught Shakespeare to thousands of students and thousands of teachers in my career, and one idea I'm constantly reminded of is readers need to be eased into Shakespeare's language. And I do mean *all* readers, be they middle school students, high school students, or even university students. I've even discovered that teachers and other adults don't react so differently from middle school students when they're first exposed to a Shakespeare play they've never read. The problem is Early Modern English (Yes, that's what it's called, not Old English or Middle English.) uses some verb endings we're not used to and sometimes uses pronouns like "thee" and "thou." But this is how people spoke in Elizabethan England (when Queen Elizabeth was on the throne, 1558–1603). Shakespeare's plays were meant to be easy for even the uneducated to understand. And no, they didn't all speak in poetry, but they had fun with the language, using colorful images and words or phrases with double meanings (some that in modern-day culture might spark some "That's what she said" responses).

I hope that, in some way, reading this book will make your experience with Shakespeare a better one, and at the same time, give you a little peek into the lives of two regular middle school kids who, through an unfortunate incident, find themselves stuck in a crazy situation. As a side note, Peter's character was inspired in some ways by Sam Schneider and Maura LoMonico, who in their early years gave me all the material I needed to make him who he is. Thanks to them for being who they are.

I also want to thank all those who encouraged me and helped launch this book through my Kickstarter campaign, especially Toby Spitzer, Kevin Costa, Peter and Maura Charles, Chris Lavold, Marcia Newell, Amy and Neal Ulen, Danette Long, William Heller, Lucille and Jim DeFeo, Judy Brown, Peggy O'Brien, and Bob Young. Thanks to those who read an early draft of this book and gave me feedback, especially Sue Kenyon, Melanie Cheda, Christina Dennis, Yaire Cort, and Zoe Joyner.

I also want to thank all those who taught me to love Shakespeare, starting with my high school students and continuing with my colleagues at the Folger Shakespeare Library, especially Peggy O'Brien and Michael Tolaydo.

And finally I want to thank Fran LoMonico, for all the love and support she has given me for so many years.

Michael LoMonico

TABLE OF CONTENTS

"WORDS, WORDS, WORDS"

Let me begin by stating that everything I'm about to tell you is true. Yes, everything. Who I am and how I came to write this book can come later. But first, let me swear that this is what actually happened.

I know you're probably not going to believe a lot of it when you hear the whole story, and I probably wouldn't believe it either if I hadn't been there to witness it all. But it's really true.

It all happened a few months ago, when I was still in eighth grade. Peter was in eighth grade, too.

Oh, I almost forgot. Peter is my friend. He's also the "Shakespeare Kid" in this book's title. The book is mainly about him. I guess it's about me, too, in a way, because of what happened between us.

We are both fourteen years old, and when all this began we were both pretty dumb when it came to girl and boy stuff. We weren't like some kids our age who were into "hanging out" and "fooling around" and other things I won't mention. Before all this happened

I had never even kissed a boy. I'm pretty sure Peter hadn't kissed any girls either. Yes, we were what you might call "nerds." But seeing what happened to a lot of those couples in our grade who were going out one week and then fighting the next week and then going out with different kids the following week, I was glad we weren't like them. We may have been nerds, but we were happy nerds.

I think I'm getting ahead of myself and saying too much already, so I'll stop. Just read the book, and you'll see what I mean.

CHAPTER ONE

"COME WHAT MAY"

P arents can be a real pain in the morning. My parents are actually pretty cool as parents go, but it's like they take pleasure in being extra annoying in the morning. Every morning my mom yells to me from the bottom of the stairs. "Emma!" she shrieks. "Time to get up!"

Oh, how I hate that. If I don't get up within five seconds, she starts singing this stupid song, "Oh, what a beautiful morning. Oh, what a beautiful day," at the top of her lungs.

Before she can get to the next line, I yell, "I'm up!" or something like that—anything to get her to stop that racket. I asked her one time where she got that song from, and she said it's from some play called *Oklahoma*. A whole play about Oklahoma? Really? Imagine what a stupid play that must be.

Peter's dad had an annoying routine for waking him up, too. And Peter hated it just as much as I hated my mom's song. "Rise and shine!" his dad would yell. That's sort of the way this crazy story starts, with Peter's dad standing over him and saying, "Rise and shine!"

According to his dad, Peter mumbled what sounded like, "*O sleep! O gentle sleep.*"

"Up and at 'em," his father responded. "It's seven o'clock, and all is well in the world."

"*Good morrow, father,*" Peter replied. Then he peeked out from under his covers and saw his father's smiling face over him. At this point his dad usually started pulling off Peter's blanket and sheets. Peter sat up quickly to avoid that, the worst part of the wake-up routine. But then he felt a little dazed and grabbed his head

His father looked worried. "Are you OK, Champ? The doctor said you might feel dizzy today. How do you feel? Do you think you should go to school?"

"*Yes, better, sir,*" Peter replied. And then he looked past his father and said, "*But soft! What light through yonder window breaks?*"

His father laughed and said, "Duh, that's the sun, and it means if you're going to school, you'll be late if you don't hurry." Peter threw the covers over his head and moaned. "Enough of this nonsense," his dad said. "Your bus will be here in half an hour."

Peter later told me that as he slowly climbed out of bed and looked at his father, he said, "*Fair thoughts and happy hours attend on you.*" As those words left his mouth, he knew something was wrong. And the look of shock on his father's face only added to his own panic.

"Say that again," his father responded. "What did you say?"

"*How like a dream is this I see and hear,*" Peter answered.

At that point, his father noticed something under the covers. Pulling back the blanket, he lifted up a fat book called *The Riverside*

Shakespeare. "Why are you sleeping with this book?" he asked. "Is this why you're talking so goofy?"

"*It is a wise father that knows his own child,*" answered Peter, surprised at his own words. He couldn't figure out what was wrong or why he kept talking so funny. He thought about the accident the day before that led to his trip to the hospital, all the tests that they had given him, and the "slight concussion" the doctor had diagnosed. He wondered if all that had anything to do with his funny way of speaking.

His father laughed and headed downstairs.

"*Half sleep, half waking: but as yet, I swear, I cannot truly say how I came here,*" Peter said to no one in particular, looking down at the book his father had left on his bed. He had only read a few pages of *Romeo and Juliet*, the play that he was studying for school, before he had fallen asleep the night before. And he didn't know much more about Shakespeare than what he'd found on Wikipedia. He'd never even seen any of Shakespeare's plays. Well, there was that version of *Macbeth* he saw on *The Simpsons*, but that didn't count.

He tried not to think about it while he took a quick shower and got dressed. "*What the dickens?*" he muttered to himself. "*Come what may.*"

He went downstairs for breakfast and noticed *Good Morning America* on TV. "*Now, what news on the Rialto?*" he asked his mom.

By now Peter's dad had told his mom their son was playing this cute word game, so she decided to roll with it. "They're going to interview the family of that young girl who was missing five years ago in the Caribbean," she said. "I honestly wish these TV people would leave these families alone."

"*All the world's a stage, and all the men and women merely players,*" Peter responded.

"I know," she said. "It seems like they almost like being on TV again. It's like they're trying to keep her memory alive."

"*What's done cannot be undone,*" Peter said.

"By the way, how do you feel this morning? I know you had quite a scare yesterday."

"*Ay, 'twas a rough night.*"

"But you feel OK to go to school?"

"*All shall be well.*"

"Well, sit down and eat your breakfast. I made bacon and eggs, your favorite."

"*I thank you. I am not a man of many words, but I thank you.*"

His mother ignored what she thought was his foolishness. I guess she was used to his wacky behavior, and this seemed to be just more of the same. "Besides," she later told me, "it was sort of fun to see what he was going to say next. I figured he couldn't keep up the game for much longer."

Peter quickly finished his breakfast, grabbed his backpack, and headed out the door. "*Parting is such sweet sorrow,*" he yelled on his way out.

CHAPTER TWO

"I WILL WEAR MY HEART UPON MY SLEEVE"

Before I continue, I need to explain a few things:

- who I am
- how Peter and I got together
- how he got his concussion
- how he began to speak so funny
- how everyone started to refer to him as "That Shakespeare Kid"

My name is Emma Malcolm, and I live down the street from Peter. We've been hanging out since he moved here three years ago, the summer before sixth grade. I remember that day so clearly. I was just sitting by the curb next to my driveway when Peter passed by on his bike. Then he turned around and stopped right in front of me.

"Hey, kid. My name is Peter. Do you wanna be friends?" he said.

"Sure. I'm Emma."

OK, I know that's not a very exciting story, but that really is how it happened. After we decided we'd be friends, he told me how old he was and that he had just moved in down the street. We then figured out we'd be going into the same grade that year, and we hung out together almost every day that summer. And when school started, we remained best friends.

Most kids at school thought Peter Marlowe was strange long before he became "That Shakespeare Kid." When you're thirteen years old, it's pretty easy to find stuff about other kids to make fun of, and Peter gave everybody lots of ammunition:

- He was one of the only boys in eighth grade named Peter, so they really gave it to him. (You can probably imagine what eighth graders would do with a name like Peter.)
- He looked a little...well, strange. He spiked his hair up with mousse each day so it resembled a porcupine. And his face was covered in freckles, which didn't help.
- He was a big fan of the cop show *Hawaii Five-0*, so in seventh grade he'd started wearing only Hawaiian shirts. His closet boasted about two dozen of them in various wild prints, and he wore one to school every day, no matter how cold it was.
- His voice was deep and raspy, sort of like a frog or an old man who had smoked three packs of cigarettes a day his whole life.
- And then he showed off all the time. He was really good at memorizing random facts, so he'd rattle off all fifty states and their capitals or the names of all the presidents and their vice presidents in order.

Not the best way to make friends, right?

He did have a few friends, though to the rest of the eighth grade, those friends were in the weirdo category, too. I guess that included me. Don't get me wrong. I'm not sorry he was my friend, and after the Shakespeare thing happened and he became famous, it was pretty cool to be his BFF and later his girlfriend. But let's not get into that now. Before I tell you any more about the Shakespeare thing, I should give you some more background.

Peter moved to Long Island when he was nine. Prior to that, he lived in New Jersey, but he hadn't liked it very much. His favorite foods were steak and pizza. He had 253 friends on Facebook, though not nearly that many in real life. He was a huge New York Mets fan. He collected baseball cards, coins, matchbooks, and lots of other stuff.

That "other stuff" is what really made him odd. Take for instance his file cabinet stage. For his thirteenth birthday, while most kids his age were asking for the latest video game console or a new dirt bike, Peter asked his parents for a metal, four-drawer, vertical file cabinet. And they gave it to him! He didn't have a real birthday party that year, but I'd been invited over for dinner that night. After dinner Peter took me to his room to show me his present.

"It's a Hon 310 series," he proudly said. "They call this color 'putty.' Isn't it beautiful?"

No, it wasn't beautiful. And it took up a big space in his tiny room. It had been placed in front of a poster of Lionel Messi, the soccer player on the Barcelona team. (Beside baseball, Peter's favorite sport was international soccer.) With the file cabinet in place, only the letters *l-o-n-a* were still visible on the poster, along with the top part of Messi's head.

"It reminds me of the color of Silly Putty," I said. "That stuff is fun to play with, but I would never call it beautiful. But, Peter, what are you going to do with it?"

"Are you kidding? There's so much organizing that needs to be done. After all, I have thirteen years worth of stuff to file."

"What kind of stuff?" I asked. "Thirteen years of what kind of stuff?"

Apparently the cabinet would help him organize his whole life chronologically. Each year would be further divided into categories, he had explained, and then rattled off a list that included:

- Every scrap of artwork he had created in preschool and kindergarten, which his mother had saved in a large box
- Everything he'd ever written, including essays, homework, reports, and even those pages and pages of printed letters of the alphabet his preschool teacher had had him practice
- A complete inventory of every book he'd ever read since the age of two, though he admitted he was disappointed his parents hadn't documented the first two years
- A complete list of every movie he'd ever seen, either in a movie theater, on TV, or on DVD, along with his own five-Marlowe rating of each one
- Maps, brochures, and bits and pieces of junk from every vacation his family had ever taken. This collection included airline ticket stubs, amusement park tickets, matchbooks, hotel stationery, and postcards, as well as placemats and menus from the restaurants they ate in.

He was teaching himself some program called Microsoft Access, which he said was a database that would streamline everything he had on file.

As he was rambling on, Mrs. Marlowe walked into the room and interrupted him. "Let me explain, Emma," she said. "He's saving all this stuff to be included in the Peter Marlowe Presidential Library someday. It's our fault," she added, "because Mr. Marlowe and I took him to see the Jimmy Carter Presidential Library when we were in Atlanta. That was when he began to categorize everything. You see, he plans to be president in forty years."

"But mom, I'm still not sure the four-drawer model will hold it all," he said. "I know it won't hold the dirt."

Ah, the dirt. Let me explain the dirt. When he was about five, Peter had started collecting, labeling, and storing dirt. That's right, dirt. He got the idea on his family's trip to Denver when he took an empty plastic film canister from his father and scooped up some red dirt and brought it back home. Since then, he was on a personal crusade to gather soil samples from every part of the United States and every part of the world. I'll never forget how excited he got when I returned from our family vacation at Atlantis on Paradise Island in the Bahamas with a bag of dirt for him. Each time he learned some of his parents' friends were traveling, he asked them to bring back some dirt. These soil donors included their doctor, who'd taken a trip to Peru; their minister, who'd gone to Iceland; their mailman, who'd taken his family to Mexico; and our middle school principal, who'd traveled to France. After a while, people who didn't even know Peter and some who'd never met the Marlowes started bringing back soil because they heard about it from others. One family friend apologized because he'd only changed planes in Sweden and had scooped some dirt from a large plant in the airport. But Peter didn't care. At this point, in his basement he had hundreds of Ziploc bags full of dirt, each carefully labeled with the date and the location from which the sample was taken. Oh, yeah, and he had one of those electric label makers, so the labels were very fancy.

Some people asked him what he was going to do with all that dirt, but he never really had an answer. It wasn't for any scientific reasons; he wasn't going to study it or put the dirt under a microscope or anything. He barely looked at it and seemed more interested in labeling and adding each bag to his collection rather than really enjoying the dirt.

"What about the newspapers?" I asked. "Where are you going to store them?"

I guess I should tell you about the newspapers, too, because that will tell you a lot about Peter. For our sixth grade project, he decided to study the American newspaper. He'd learned about this organization called Newspapers in Education, and I guess that's what got him started. He emailed about a hundred daily newspapers that were part of that program and requested a sample print copy from each. He made sure he had at least one from each state. His idea was to compare them on some sort of chart. Well, pretty soon they started to arrive in his mailbox. He averaged about five newspapers a day, and several of the papers actually sent their Sunday editions— ads and all. Peter hadn't quite planned ahead, and suddenly there were papers piling up in his room and then in his basement. After about two weeks, he decided the project was kind of wacky and out of control. He even had trouble facing our angry mail deliverer each day. Instead of that project, he requested an in-person interview with the editor of *Newsday*, the Long Island daily paper. He actually got the interview and based his project around that, but the papers continued arriving in his mailbox each day for several more weeks.

"So, what are you doing with the papers?" I repeated.

"Mr. Marlowe and Peter loaded up our minivan last year and took them all to be recycled," his mother broke in. "Peter wanted to hold onto them for some possible future project, but we had to do something about them. They were taking over the house."

Peter continued to look at his prized birthday gift, the Hon 310. Then he proudly announced, "I'm calling it the Great Cabinet of Wonders." His mom and I just shook our heads.

As I said before, Peter really liked baseball. He'd played Little League since he was nine, but he wasn't very good. He was far more interested in keeping the statistics than playing the game. He learned how to use an official scorecard from the start, and for each game he recorded, he included attendance and weather. He created a spreadsheet each season to tabulate such things as everyone's batting and fielding averages as well as the pitchers' earned run averages. If you asked him, he could even supply stats such as on-base and slugging percentages. Unfortunately, his own numbers in most categories were pretty low, but his coach and his teammates appreciated his scorekeeping—sort of.

And then there was the fantasy baseball league he joined with his pediatrician and seven other doctors from the local hospital. How he managed to get involved with these guys is a long story not worth repeating. But suffice it to say his parents dropped him off every Sunday morning in the local diner to meet with these doctors to discuss trades and all that other fantasy baseball stuff. Apparently, they originally thought inviting him would be a cute idea and he would stop coming after one or two sessions. But they soon found out how knowledgeable and competitive he was, and for the next two years he was a regular on the team.

But after the Shakespeare thing happened and Peter started saying things like "*A horse! A horse! My kingdom for a horse*," "*I will wear my heart upon my sleeve*," and "*O brave new world that has such people in't*" life got even more nuts.

CHAPTER THREE

"TO SLEEP: PERCHANCE TO DREAM"

So now back to the story of how Peter became "That Shakespeare Kid." Here's how it all began.

On Thursday, April 15, our English teacher, Ms. Hastings, told us we'd be reading Shakespeare's *Romeo and Juliet* in class. She handed out really old copies of the play along with book receipts to make sure we returned our copies. Like we were going to steal these dirty old books. I filled out my receipt, and on the line that said "Book Condition" I wrote "awful." It was missing the back cover, and the pages were all worn. Gross. As we were leaving class, she told us to read Act 1 for homework.

Like most of us, Peter had never read or seen a Shakespeare play before, but as soon as he found out we'd be reading one, he went into high gear. When he got home, he got on Wikipedia and searched for "Shakespeare." Here's what he found:

William Shakespeare (26 April 1564 (baptised) – 23 April 1616) was an English poet and playwright, widely regarded as the greatest writer in the English language and the world's pre-eminent dramatist.[1] He is often called England's national poet and the "Bard of Avon". His extant works, including some collaborations, consist of about 38 plays, 154 sonnets, two long narrative poems, and a few other verses, the authorship of some of which is uncertain. His plays have been translated into every major living language and are performed more often than those of any other playwright.

Shakespeare was born and brought up in Stratford-upon-Avon. At the age of 18, he married Anne Hathaway, with whom he had three children: Susanna, and twins Hamnet and Judith. Between 1585 and 1592, he began a successful career in London as an actor, writer, and part owner of a playing company called the Lord Chamberlain's Men, later known as the King's Men. He appears to have retired to Stratford around 1613 at age 49, where he died three years later.

What followed was more information about the plays and sonnets he wrote and lots of links and other bits and pieces about Shakespeare.

Peter texted me to see if I wanted to go over to his house, so we could do our homework together. We didn't always do that, especially if the homework was easy, but this looked like it was going to be a lot harder. I went right over with my tattered copy of *Romeo and Juliet* and was ready to get started, but Peter wasn't.

"I want to get a better copy of the play," he said. "Mine's really bad."

"So is mine. What difference does it make?"

"It makes a big difference. I want a good copy, and I think my mom has one in her study."

His parents were both still at work, so I was a little worried we might get in trouble for snooping in his mom's room. But we went into the room he called the "study." I'd been to his house a lot of times, but we'd never been in that room. I'd never even heard of a room called a study. We didn't have one in my house, and I was curious. It was a small room with stacks and stacks of books on gray bookshelves, which covered one wall and nearly reached the ceiling. There was a grand, wooden desk and a small, brown leather couch in the room as well. As I looked over the room, Peter found what he was looking for.

"There it is," he said, pointing. "It's that big, brown book on the top shelf. I remember my mother called it *The Riverside Shakespeare.* She used it in college, and it contains all the plays and poems Shakespeare wrote."

"So, how do you plan on getting it down?"

"Watch this," he said. I laughed as he rolled the desk chair over to the shelf. It was one of those chairs with wheels and a reclining back, but he stood on it anyway. "This will be easy," he said. "Just hold the chair."

When he climbed onto the chair, it became a little unsteady. And when he stretched his fingers out to dislodge the heavy book, the wheels of the chair started to move. I tried to steady it, but the book came tumbling down and hit Peter's head, throwing his balance off even more. He screamed out, and then he, the book, and the chair crashed to the ground. His head hit the desk on the way down, and his legs got caught under the chair. Then he stopped moving. I tried to shake him awake, but it didn't work.

I panicked. I tried shaking him again, but to no avail. I don't know why, but I immediately called my mother at her office. "Mom, I'm over at Peter's house, and he fell, and now he's unconscious! I don't know what to do!"

"Calm down, Emma. Stop crying, and tell me what happened," she responded.

I told her about the book and the chair. She told me to call 9-1-1 and she'd be right over. Her office was pretty close by, so I knew she'd only be about five minutes.

By the time I got the emergency dispatcher on the line, Peter's eyes were half open, and he was just lying there groaning. I told the dispatcher what had happened and must have sounded scared because she kept telling me to talk slowly and stay calm. Why is it when something bad happens, everyone tells you to stay calm? When I hear that, I get even more upset. I gave her Peter's address, and she asked me a bunch more questions. She said the EMTs would be over right away.

When I got off the phone, Peter was looking at me. "Are you all right?" I asked. He said nothing, almost like he didn't hear me. His eyes rolled around and seemed to have trouble focusing.

I went to his room and found his cell phone on his bed. I looked through his contacts, found one labeled "MOMS OFF," and figured it was Mrs. Marlowe's office. I knew she worked in New York City and wouldn't be able to get there right away, but I called her anyway. Here's our conversation:

"Hi, Mrs. Marlowe. This is Emma."

"Hi, Emma. Where's Peter?"

"Uh, he's right here, but there was a little accident."

"An accident? What happened? Let me talk to him."

"He really can't talk now, but he's all right."

"If he's all right, why can't I talk to him?"

"Well, you see, he fell and hit his head. But I called 9-1-1, and the EMTs are on their way."

"EMTs? Oh my god! What happened?"

"He was trying to get a book down from the top shelf in your study, and he fell and hit his head. But he's not bleeding or anything. My mother is coming over now."

"OK. Look, I'm in the city, but I'll be on the next train home. Mr. Marlowe also works downtown,

but we'll both get there as soon as we can. But it probably won't be for over an hour."

"OK."

"But call me as soon as the EMTs get there and let me know what's what."

"Sure. Look, Mrs. Marlowe, I'm so sorry. I wish I could have stopped him from falling."

"Don't worry about that, Emma. Just stay with him. I'm on my way right now."

I ended the call and looked over at Peter, whose demeanor hadn't changed. I ran to the bathroom and got him a glass of water because I didn't know what else to do. I was a wreck because I probably should have held the chair better for him. I kept asking him if there was anything else I could do, but he only shook his head.

It seemed like hours had gone by when I finally heard sirens and went to the door to let the EMTs in. There were two of them, a man and a woman. "My name is Maria, and his name is Frank," the female EMT said to me. "What's your name, and how did this happen?"

I told her my name and about the book and the chair, and they immediately jumped into action. They took Peter's blood pressure and pulse and did so many other things I can't even remember. They even gave him oxygen. All the while Peter didn't say anything.

After a while, Maria asked me again what had happened, but she didn't seem satisfied with my explanation of the accident. Then she asked me the most unbelievable question. "Listen, Emma. Just between us, were you two using drugs when this happened?"

I was so shocked I just stood there and couldn't even answer at first. If she knew Peter and me, she never would have asked that question. Finally, I just said, "Are you kidding? No way!"

"Listen," she responded. "I'm only here to help, so if there's anything you need to tell me, please do it now."

I didn't know what to say, so I just walked away. Fortunately, that's when my mother arrived. I had been pretty strong up to that point, but when I saw her I started crying. The tears just flowed. My mom held me tight and kept telling me it was OK.

By then, Peter was sitting up and seemed a little better, though he still wasn't talking. The EMTs told my mom they were taking him to the hospital. Maria called Mrs. Marlowe and told her Peter was stable and that my mom and I would ride in the ambulance with him to Stony Brook Hospital. Mr. and Mrs. Marlowe should meet us there.

As the EMTs got Peter onto the stretcher, he looked up and said, "*For this relief, much thanks.*" That remark was a bit strange, but I was too upset then to even think about it at the time. Only later did I realize that that moment marked the beginning of Peter's "disorder."

Peter was silent in the ambulance. I was scared, but I still thought it was pretty cool to be riding in an ambulance with the siren blaring. Suddenly Peter sat up and said, "*Alack, what noise is this?*" I told him it was the siren and we were headed to the hospital. He closed his eyes again and lay back down.

We zipped through traffic and got to the hospital in what seemed like record time. When we pulled in, I expected a team of doctors and nurses to be waiting outside, just like on TV. But no one was there, except some woman smoking and a security guard who barely noticed us. The EMTs opened the ambulance door and wheeled Peter into the ER.

My Mom and I followed the stretcher, and she told the woman behind the desk that Peter's parents were on their way. Apparently, the doctors couldn't really give him any medicine or do much before his parents got there, but an ER nurse wheeled him to a small room and took his blood pressure and other vitals. When she told him his blood pressure was a bit high at 140 over 90, he said, "*I am ill at these numbers.*" We all laughed at that, and when the Emergency Room doctor asked him how he felt, he simply said, "*Madam, I am not well.*"

She pulled the curtain closed and said we could sit down and wait until his parents got there. Peter fell asleep, and my mom and I sat there, not saying much to each other. After a long time, his parents arrived together. Mrs. Marlowe gave me a big hug and thanked my mother and me for everything we'd done.

"I'm so sorry this happened," I said, as I started to cry again.

"Don't be silly," she said. "I'm sure it's not your fault. It sounds like something Peter would do, and I'm just glad you were there. I can't imagine what would've happened if he'd been alone when he fell."

Soon after, my dad came to the hospital to drive my mom and me home. I was exhausted and cried all the way.

Mrs. Marlowe called us around ten that night and told us they'd just gotten home. She said the doctors had taken some brain scans and run a few other tests and that Peter was diagnosed with a "slight concussion." She thanked me for keeping "a cool head" and again assured me it was not my fault he'd fallen. She said he was still a bit dizzy but would probably be going to school the next day to keep up his perfect record.*

Later I found out that when they got home and his mother suggested he get right to bed, Peter nodded and said, "*To sleep: perchance to dream; ay, there's the rub.*"

Let me tell you about his "record." Peter was so proud of the fact he'd never missed a day of school—not even when he was in preschool at Miss Sue's School. He rarely got sick, and even if he did, he dragged himself to class. His goal was to make it through high school with a perfect attendance record. When I asked him if there was some sort of award he was trying to win, he'd just laughed and said he was doing it because it was hard.

CHAPTER FOUR

"SO BETHUMPED WITH WORDS"

The next day was warm for the middle of April. I was already at the bus stop a few doors down from Peter's house when I saw him coming. You couldn't miss him, wearing a bright orange Hawaiian shirt.

"Hey, Peter," I said when he got there. "I was so worried about you. Are you feeling better today?"

He hesitated awhile, and then responded *"Methinks I see these things with parted eye."* He looked surprised at himself, like he didn't know where the words had come from.

"What are you talking about? I asked.

"But soft, methinks I scent the morning air," he said.

"Huh? Start making sense."

"All the world is cheered by the sun."

"Very funny. Methinks you're an idiot."

"Go Rot!"

"What's with you and this stupid way of talking?"

"*I never was so bethumped with words. 'Tis my occupation to be plain.*"

"Listen, Peter," I said, annoyed. "You're really starting to get on my nerves."

"*Alack*," was his only reply.

Just then the bus pulled up. "Well, methinks I'll be sitting as far away from you as I can on the bus. You're really creeping me out," I said.

Peter avoided all conversation on the bus, which wasn't very hard because, except for me, he really didn't have many friends. I usually found Peter's oddness to be fun. But that morning I was still getting over the fall and the ambulance and the hospital, and I just wasn't in the mood for his goofiness. So I sat next to my friend Melanie, and Peter sat in the front seat behind the driver—alone.

When Peter got into school he kept quiet. He just shook his head when Mr. Scott, his math teacher, asked him if he'd done his homework. Of course he had done his homework, but if he'd tried to say "Yes," he may have blurted out something like, "*Shall we go draw our numbers and set on?*" He did the same thing in Social Studies because if Ms. Delaney had asked him a question, he might have said, "*To be or not to be. That is the question.*"

He wasn't the kind of student who just sat in the back and kept quiet, so when I saw him that afternoon, he looked frustrated. He was sitting alone in study hall when I walked in and sat across from him. "You don't look too good," I said. "Are you feeling all right?"

"*I am not merry*," said Peter.

"Well that's OK, but I hope you're not still talking that dumb way you were this morning," I said. "I don't know what you were trying to prove."

"*Why, 'tis good to be sad and say nothing.*"

34

"Huh? Not again. Why are you acting so lame? What do you have to be sad about?"

"*In sooth, I know not why I am so sad. I have this while with leaden thoughts been pressed.*"

"So you don't know why you're talking so funny, and you don't know why you're depressed? Well, if you ask me, start talking like a normal person and see if that helps."

"*Say, why is this? Wherefore? What should we do?*"

I shook my head and walked away despite Peter's desperate cry after me: "*Anon!*"

During lunch that day, Peter ran down to the library and got on the first computer he could find. He went right to Google and carefully typed in the exact phrase he'd said to me earlier: "*In sooth I know not why I am so sad.*" A list of links popped up, he clicked on the first one, and it took him to Act 1 Scene 1 of a Shakespeare play called *The Merchant of Venice.* He recalled some of the other things he'd said that morning and one-by-one entered what he could remember into Google. "*What's done cannot be undone*" was from *Macbeth;* "*All the world's a stage*" came from *As You Like It;* and "*Methinks I scent the morning air*" was a line from *Hamlet.* They were all Shakespeare's plays!

"*Zounds!*" he shouted, "*I am fortune's fool!*" Every head in the relatively quiet library turned toward Peter. He didn't pay them any attention, though, because he'd finally figured out what he'd been saying. Every word out of his mouth was a line from one of Shakespeare's plays.

But he still had no idea why he was doing it. And even worse, no matter how hard he tried, he couldn't stop quoting Shakespeare. He logged off the computer and slowly walked out of the library.

He entered the cafeteria, got in line, told the cafeteria lady what he wanted by pointing to a grilled cheese sandwich and fries, and grabbed himself a container of milk.

The cashier took his money and gave him change. "Thank you, and have a great day!" she said.

Peter usually gave this lady a warm response, but that day he just mumbled, "*I thank you for your honest care,*" under his breath.

After lunch, Peter stopped at his locker to pick up his copy of *Romeo and Juliet* for English class. Ms. Hastings was his favorite teacher, and although he hadn't gotten too far with his homework the night before, he'd been looking forward to starting the play in class.

Ms. Hastings had a habit of standing by the classroom door and greeting each student as he or she entered. I sat just inside the door and was already seated when Peter came into the room. I heard his and Ms. Hastings's conversation from my seat.

"Good afternoon, Peter," she said. "How are you today?"

"*Good day and happiness,*" Peter answered, thinking this class might be a safe place to speak.

"Are you ready for some English?" Ms. Hastings sang (in the same way they used to start *Monday Night Football*).

"*The readiness is all,*" he answered.

Ms. Hastings barely noticed his remarks, as she was busy greeting the next kid with the same corny line she used every day. Peter, looking only a little better than he had at lunch, took his seat.

After taking attendance and passing back an old quiz, Ms. Hastings told us to open our books to the first scene in *Romeo and Juliet*. "I'm sure you all noticed the play starts with this guy called the Chorus who comes out and speaks to the audience. Who can tell me what happens in the Prologue?"

She was answered with dead silence that lasted nearly a minute. She repeated the question and then started to call on individual kids to respond.

I looked over at Peter and saw he was in a panic. I gave him a strange look and then glanced down at my tattered copy of *Romeo and Juliet* and read the first line to myself: "*Two Households, both alike in dignity, in fair Verona where we lay our scene...*" I glanced back at Peter and saw he was mouthing those very words, followed by, "*From ancient grudge break to new mutiny, where civil blood makes civil hands unclean...*" I could also see he was about to raise his hand. To stop him from embarrassing himself, I quickly raised mine. Ms. Hastings looked pleased and said, "Thank you, Emma. Please tell us what the Prologue is about." I explained the Prologue described the situation in this town in Italy where these two stupid families have been feuding and these two jerky kids fall in love but can't get it together and so kill themselves. When I finished, I looked over at Peter. He seemed relieved he was off the hook.

But suddenly, Abby, who clearly hadn't done her homework, was yelling at me. "They die in the end? You just ruined the whole story, Emma," she said. "What's the point of reading this if we know how it's going to end?" Several other kids thought this was a good opportunity to start a campaign against reading Shakespeare, so they loudly agreed with her.

Ms. Hastings tried to calm them by explaining that Shakespeare's plots weren't the only reason we read his plays and that most of his plots weren't even original.

"You mean he used other people's stories?" Brian asked. "Isn't that what you called...that 'p' word? Isn't that plagiarism?"

Grumbles among the students signaled another protest was about to start.

"No, no. Everyone settle down and let me explain," Ms. Hastings said. "Shakespeare is about the beauty of words. Notice how he wrote '*a pair of star-crossed lovers*' rather than 'two jerky kids,' which is what Emma called them. Doesn't Shakespeare sound better? But before we actually start to read this play," she continued, "we need to know all about Shakespeare's life. Who can tell me something about him?"

As Ms. Hastings went on about Shakespeare, I could see that Peter, along with the rest of us, was tuning out. But then we all heard the magic words—"This *will* be on the quiz!"—and frantically began taking notes. At that point, Peter noticed that not only his thoughts were in normal English, but so was his writing. That's when the texting started.

Hearing my phone vibrate, I slowly took it out of my backpack and read: emma, i have a ? 4 u. :(

It was from Peter and he meant, "I have a question for you." Here's how the rest of the exchange went:

Emma: yes?

Peter: r u my friend?

Emma: yes

Peter: ok. i can't talk right. every time i try, i quote shakespeare.

Emma: that's what u were doing at the bus stop?

Peter: yes. i can't help it. i can think n write normal, but i can't stop talking funny.

Emma: really?

Peter: yes. i googled some of what i said, n they were all lines from shakespeare. from all different plays. u have 2 help me.

I looked up to see if Ms. Hastings had noticed we were texting, but she was saying something about Shakespeare's will and his "second-best bed" and wasn't paying attention to us. So I texted back:

Emma: what do u want me 2 do?

Peter: i need you 2 speak 4 me. i'll text u n u say it out loud 4 me. ok?

Emma: i like you n all, but this sounds stupid. r u fooling w/ me?

Peter: no, i swear.

Emma: ok...

Peter: :)

I looked up, and Ms. Hastings was drawing a funny picture of the Globe Theatre on the board when Peter texted me again: ugh.

when we study a book she tells us all about the writer's life. like that's going 2 help us understand or get us 2 like it.

While I was reading the text Tim, the class wise guy, said, "My father said he saw this movie that proved Shakespeare didn't even write those plays. So why do we even have to read this stuff?"

Ms. Hastings seemed to be expecting that question. "Ah, yes," she replied. "I get this question each year. Those people who claim William Shakespeare didn't write these plays say that because we know Shakespeare never went to college. You see, they had really good records at the only two colleges in England at that time, Cambridge and Oxford. And his name is nowhere to be found in their records. So these people find someone who *did* go to college and say *that* person must have written the plays. It's sort of snobbery. Besides, what they don't think about is maybe Shakespeare was a genius and going to college wasn't necessary for him."

"Hey, we're in the gifted class," said Tim. "Does that mean we don't have to go to college?"

"There's a big difference between being gifted and being a genius," she said. "So let's get back to work, or you'll never even get to ninth grade."

Before I realized what I was doing, I raised my hand and interrupted Ms. Hastings's description of Shakespeare's birthplace. I said what Peter had texted me: "Will this stuff about Shakespeare's life and the Globe Theater actually help us understand *Romeo and Juliet*?" And that's how I became Peter's spokesperson. Whenever he wanted to say something normal, he texted it to me, and I said it out loud.

Even though Ms. Hastings was prepared to answer questions about who wrote the plays or the fact that the stories Shakespeare told weren't new, she had evidently never heard Peter's question before. She was speechless for a moment, and then quietly said, "Well, Emma. It won't directly help you understand the play, but it's important to know all about this."

Peter texted me again, and I repeated it to Ms. Hastings. "Why?" I asked as politely as I could.

She seemed a bit angry with that, even though I hadn't said it rudely and she and I had always gotten along. "It's part of what everyone needs to know," she said. "If you don't know where Shakespeare was born or how many children he had or what the Globe Theater looked like…" Then the weirdest thing happened. She stopped midsentence, looked down at her desk, and after a long pause, told us to read Act 1 in our books silently at our seats.

I didn't think she was mad at me, but I could tell she was upset. The class didn't know what to think, and those last twenty minutes leading up to the bell were the quietest I ever remember kids being in any class.

When the bell rang, Ms. Hastings told me to stay behind so she could talk to me. I wasn't quite sure what to do. I didn't know if I was in trouble for asking Peter's stupid question or if maybe she'd seen me using my phone. If I told her about the texting scheme, and that it was really Peter asking the question, we'd both get in trouble for using our cell phones in class. The school rule about that was pretty clear, and the punishment was a one-day suspension. I could already imagine my parents' reaction when they found out. I'd probably be grounded, and I would definitely lose my phone for a long time.

As I waited for the room to empty out, I noticed Peter standing in the back. Was he going to tell her everything? But then she looked at me and said, "Emma, I'm not angry at you for asking that question. It was a good question, but I'm not sure I can answer it without thinking a lot about it over the weekend. I'll get back to you on Monday."

Wow, was I relieved. And Peter, who overheard all this, was smiling when we left the room. He gave me a high five and said, "*To conclude, the victory fell on us!*"

"Sure," I said as I walked away from him. "Whatever."

CHAPTER FIVE

"THE GAME IS AFOOT!"

Peter IM'd me that night to tell me the latest. Even though he'd spoken some Shakespeare lines to his mom and dad that morning, they really hadn't figured out what was happening. So he wrote them a note explaining he couldn't control himself, and that he could only speak Shakespeare. Of course, they didn't believe him at first. He said they finally did when he actually started crying and said, "*Doubt thou the stars are fire; doubt that the sun doth move; doubt truth to be a liar; but never doubt I love.*"

Once they realized he wasn't faking it, they seemed really scared, he explained. They made a quick call to his old pediatrician, but she didn't have anything to say other than it sounded like it had to do with the concussion and would certainly pass. She said to wait a few more days, and if it continued they should see a neurologist. They asked the doctor about a speech therapist, but she convinced them to take one step at a time. Peter's parents also said they'd go to school Monday and explain it to the principal. I told him it would be all right soon, and he responded, *"Good night, good night! parting is such sweet sorrow, that I shall say good night till it be morrow."*

But about an hour later, he texted me:

Peter: want 2 go 2 the mets game tmrw?

Emma: sure. what's the deal?

Peter: my dad has tickets n they are good seats right next 2 the dugout

Emma: great. i have 2 check w/ my parents but they will be cool with it

Peter: maybe it will make me 4get this stupid shakespeare speak

Emma: i hope so

I figured his father thought this would help Peter be distracted and maybe even shake him out of his condition. I was really excited about going because they were playing the Nationals, their biggest rival, and Peter's dad had these great box seats from his company. Besides, he always bought us lots of food and souvenirs at games.

Peter was a huge fan and could usually give out all kinds of stats, but with his new way of talking, I knew this game was going to be really bizarre. Mr. Marlowe had to do some work at his office before the game, so he'd drive his car into the city that morning and park it at the stadium. Peter and I were going to take the train to the stadium and meet him there.

My parents weren't too happy with this plan, but Peter's dad called and assured them we'd be fine. We'd taken the train into the city alone three times before—once when his dad had floor seats to the Knicks, once when he had tickets to see the *Lion King* on Broadway, and one Mets game the year before.

When he came over to my house the next morning, Peter was wearing a bright Hawaiian shirt sporting the Mets' colors, orange and blue. My mom dropped us off at the station, and while we waited, Peter and I didn't say much to each other. He only spoke once, when he looked down the track and saw the train: "*The train approacheth.*"

He was preoccupied on the train ride and not that excited about the game. He had a small notepad with him and began writing me notes.

> *I'm sorry I had to text you in class yesterday and IM you last night instead of talking, but I still can't talk without speaking like Shakespeare.*

I took the notepad from him and was about to write a reply, but he snatched it back from me.

I Can Hear,

he wrote in big letters.

You can just speak to me.

"Oh, right," I said. "Do you have any idea about why you're talking like Shakespeare?"

He scribbled NO.

"Does it have to do with that book falling on your head?" I asked.

"*That book in many's eyes doth share the glory,*" he said, staring out the window miserably.

"Don't worry," I said. "We'll figure this out. And it'll be a great game."

He turned back to the notepad and wrote,

> I'm still trying to talk as little as possible to them. When my dad asked me about the game, all I could say was

"*I can no other answer make but thanks.*" He spoke the last part.

We remained quiet the rest of the ride.

The train was crowded with Mets fans, and as the Mets' stadium, CitiField, came into view, an older guy started to bang a stick on this old, dented cowbell. He was wearing a Mets shirt with the name "COWBELL MAN" on the back. The fans on the train all started yelling and chanting, "Let's go, Mets! Let's go, Mets!" But Peter, who normally would have been standing on his seat and leading the cheer, just sat quietly staring out the window.

"Are you OK?" I asked. "You seem depressed again."

"*Methinks nobody should be sad but I,*" he said, turning to look at me.

"Huh?" I replied. "Aren't you excited about seeing the Mets? They're in second place, you know. So what gives? Why are you so down?"

With that he slowly turned to look out the scratchy window again. "*They that pitch will be defiled,*" he said slowly.

"Harvey's pitching today," I said. "What does 'defiled' mean? Do you think the Mets are going to lose?"

"*A foregone conclusion,*" was all he said.

"Sure, whatever," I said, not quite sure what was going on in his mind.

The train arrived at CitiField, and the crowd made its way down the stairs and through the crowded exit. We found Peter's dad in the crowd as we left the station. We made our way toward the entrance, which is called the Jackie Robinson Rotunda, and I could see Cowbell Man up ahead—or I should say I *heard* him?—still banging his bell and leading the cheer, "Let's go, Mets! Let's go, Mets!" Peter seemed a little better. He clapped along with the crowd and yelled, "*Strike upon the bell! Strike upon the bell!*"

We had to get in a long line where they searched our bags. Unlike some places where they search you to make sure you don't bring in your own snacks, these security people are only interested in looking for weapons and bombs, not hero sandwiches and peanuts. We waited in line for what seemed like forever, and I thought Peter had probably figured out there was a more efficient way of running this type of security, so he was especially annoyed. When we finally got through the security check, Peter turned to me and said, "*Lord, what fools these mortals be.*" I just nodded and smiled.

I always get excited when I enter the stadium. The grass seems so green, and there is a real sense of excitement in the air. CitiField is so much nicer and cleaner than the old Shea Stadium, but just like in Shea, they still have a big red apple in centerfield that pops up whenever a Met hits a home run. With the help of an usher we found our seats, and they were fantastic—in the first row, right next to the Mets dugout. We could even hear the players' comments to each other as they prepared to take the field. Peter had bought a scorecard and got busy writing in the players' names.

Mr. Marlowe waved his arm and an actual waitress came over and asked us what we wanted to eat. She gave us these printed menus, and Peter's dad said we could order whatever we wanted. "*O, I die for food!*" said Peter. I showed him the menu and told him to point to what he wanted. I ordered burgers and fries and chocolate shakes from Shake Shack for both of us. The food came in about ten minutes, and it was really good. Then a New York City police officer was introduced to sing the National Anthem. Pretty soon after, the Mets took the field, the crowd roared, and the umpire yelled out that familiar cry, "Play ball!"

As the first Nationals player came up to bat, Peter yelled out, "*The game is afoot!*" Some guys behind us laughed, but I just sank down in my seat.

The Nationals went down in order, and the Mets came to bat. The leadoff batter got a single, and Peter shouted out, "*A hit! A hit! A very palpable hit.*" Some of the fans around us laughed and so did Peter's dad. Even the guy on deck turned around to see who'd said it. The inning continued, and the next batter also hit a single, moving the guy on first base to third. The next batter hit a long fly ball to center field, setting up a sacrifice. Peter was ready for that play and screamed out, "*Hence! Home...get you home*," to the guy on third. And the player scored the first run. I began sinking down lower in my seat. Peter was really embarrassing me. His dad was busy talking to some guy from his office, who was also in the box, and wasn't paying Peter much attention at all.

The next batter drew a walk on four pitches, and then there were two men on base. The following batter hit a foul pop-up that headed our way. "*I shall catch the fly*," yelled Peter. As the ball came closer, he added, "*I'll catch it ere it come to ground.*" But the ball dropped off to our right. "*Alack*," he said. Then that batter hit a long line drive down the right field line, and Peter yelled out, "*O, 'tis fair!*" But the umpire called it a foul ball, to which Peter hollered, "*Fair is foul, and foul is fair!*"

After that, I took that notepad he'd used on the train and started writing down what he was saying. (After keeping that notepad for a few days, I got the idea to write this book about him and how this all happened.) Here are some of the things he said during the game:

- When a Mets player hit a home run, which made the Big Apple in center field pop up: "*What, up and down, carved like an apple.*"
- When the crowd was cheering for that Met who got a home run, Peter pointed to the stands and said: "*Alack. Full of sound and fury.*"
- When the leadoff batter scored later in the game: "*He comes the third time home.*"
- When the Mets' leading hitter struck out for the third time: "*Have all his ventures failed? What, not one hit?*"

- When a Met struck out with bases loaded: "*Now you strike like the blind man.*"
- When a rookie relief pitcher came in for the Nats: "*He hath a lean and hungry look.*"
- When he was encouraging one of the Mets to steal second base: "*Taste your legs, sir; put them in motion.*"
- Every time a player from either team got four balls: "*You may go walk.*"
- When a Met was caught stealing second base: "*Where shall I find one that can steal well?*"
- When he saw a Met attempting to steal a base and wanted him to stay put: "*You have scarce time to steal.*"
- When the Mets pitcher threw a ball over the catcher's head: "*Stinking pitch.*"
- When one of the Mets did a great job of rounding the bases: "*As swift in motion as a ball.*"
- When the Mets shortstop missed an easy ground ball: "*That one error fills him with faults.*"
- When another Met dropped an easy fly ball: "*O hateful error.*"
- When a Nats player slid into home while the ball was still in the outfield: "*The fool slides.*"
- When the Mets center fielder struck out with bases loaded and two outs to lose the game: "*This was the most unkindest cut of all.*"
- And as we left the stadium, when I turned to him and said I was so sorry the Mets had lost: "*Ay, that way goes the game.*"

People sitting around us had stopped laughing at Peter's lines after the second inning. I was so embarrassed because many of them kept looking at us. Of course, they had no idea why he was yelling out all these strange phrases, but it really was distracting. I was glad to be busy writing everything down.

We all were pretty upset walking to the car, Peter and his dad because of the loss, but I was upset because of Peter. I desperately wanted to talk to Mr. Marlowe about Peter's condition on the car ride home, and I'm sure he wanted to discuss it with me. But we remained quiet. The only remark Peter made was when we got into the car. He simply said, *"What's done is done."*

And then I turned away and whispered to myself, "I'm done with you, Peter."

CHAPTER SIX

"PARTING IS SUCH SWEET SORROW"

When I walked into my house that night, I went right into my room and broke down crying. I guess I'd been holding it back all day and hadn't wanted to cry in front of Peter or his father. But deep inside I was a mess. Ever since the accident, I'd been crying on and off.

My mom came up to my room, hugged me, and asked what had happened. It took me a while to stop crying, and by then my dad had come in as well. When I finally stopped blubbering, I told my parents the whole story about Peter, starting with everything that happened in school Friday and what went on at the ball game. They knew Peter pretty well, so they assumed it was a big joke he was carrying too far.

I found myself defending him. "He really can't help himself," I said. "And it's all my fault because I didn't hold the chair for him, and that stupid book hit him on the head."

"First of all," said my dad, "it's not your fault. And second, I want you to stay away from him. He's always been wacky, and I think he's a bad influence on you. You're a bright young woman. You need to make some other friends and forget him."

I was still sniffling a little, but I realized my dad was probably right. Before all this started, I was starting to really like Peter, but I couldn't take what was going on now.

My mother, the peacemaker, interrupted. "How about we all go out to dinner?" she said. She always used food as a solution. "What are you in the mood for, Emma? We could go to Applebee's or that new Italian place."

"Can't we just bring home a pizza or something?" I asked through more sniffling. "I really want to stay home tonight." I certainly didn't want to be at a restaurant smiling like everything was OK.

And so we ordered in.

Later that night, Peter sent me a text: emma, sorry i acted like a jerk 2day.

I looked at my phone for a long time. I didn't know what to do. He was saying he was sorry and admitting he was a jerk. I thought this might be a good time to tell him I didn't want to hang out with him anymore, but I really *did* want to hang out with him. I was so confused. While I was still trying to decide how to respond, he sent the same message, this time in all caps: SORRY I ACTED LIKE A JERK 2DAY.

I finally texted him back: that's OK but i was really upset. every1 was looking @ us n laughing @ u.

Peter: i'm sorry. but i always yell stuff @ games n i couldn't help myself. it woulda been hard 2 keep quiet the whole time.

Emma: i told my parents what happened in school n @ the game. they r upset.

Peter: i guess u had 2. my dad really gave it 2 me, but i wrote him a note n told him i can't help it. my mom just cried a lot.

Emma: ok i 4give you, but u have 2 get help.

Peter: i know.

Emma: what r ur parents going 2 do?

Peter: we have an appointment with a shrink next week.

Emma: great. i hope that helps.

Peter: could u come with me n read all my texts for the shrink? please?

Emma: hold on. brb.

I didn't know how to respond. I thought about the conversation I had had with my parents that night, and I knew they might be right. Peter had almost gotten me into real trouble in school and had made going to the game a terrible time. But I knew he really needed me. Finally I texted him back: OK. c u monday. goodnight.

Then Peter responded in a full sentence: Good night, good night! Parting is such sweet sorrow, that I shall say good night till it be morrow.

So, that's how I got involved.

CHAPTER SEVEN

"O, I AM SLAIN!"

I kept my phone off and avoided the computer all day Sunday, because as much as I wanted to be there for Peter, I really needed a break.

Monday morning, as our bus pulled away from our street, it was clear his condition hadn't improved. "*Prithee, speak, how many score of miles may we well ride 'twixt hour and hour?*" were the first words out of his mouth. He then texted me that his parents were going to see the principal after school. They wanted to know if I could go along to translate for Peter. I said I would.

When we were walking into the school, he said, "*There is much matter to be heard and learn'd.*" Later, when we walked into the cafeteria, he said, "*Mine eyes smell onions; I shall weep anon.*" I knew he couldn't help himself, but I was getting more annoyed by the minute.

All day I thought about English, my only class with Peter. I wondered if Ms. Hastings was going to answer my question—or actually,

Peter's question—and if he would be texting me like a maniac again. As I walked into the classroom, I noticed Ms. Hastings had a huge smile on her face. The bell rang, and she began to speak. "Class, remember on Friday when Emma asked me if studying Shakespeare's life would help us understand *Romeo and Juliet?* Well, after thinking about it over the weekend, I did some searching and decided to try a different approach. We're not going to just read Shakespeare; we're going to perform Shakespeare!"

You can imagine the groans that came from the class, including mine.

"Thanks a lot, Emma," someone said.

Ms. Hastings continued, telling us we were going to start slowly, but that by the time we finished *Romeo and Juliet,* we'd be performing whole scenes in class. And we might even get to perform our scenes for the whole school at a Shakespeare Festival. She pulled out some books, and we began our Shakespeare journey.

Peter sent me a simple text: COOL. I smiled back at him but didn't text him. I wanted to see what would happen next.

Ms. Hastings gave each of us a piece of paper with three columns of words on it. The columns were labeled *A, B,* and *C.* The top of the page explained that these were Shakespearean insults and that we should make up our own. The instructions were to pick one word from column *A,* one from column *B,* and one from column *C* and then to get up and wander around the room and "greet" each other with "Thou" and then the three-word phrase.

I looked over the list and came up with mine: *Thou hideous, rump-fed clotpole!* I didn't know what a *clotpole* was, but it sounded really gross. Ms. Hastings told us all to get up and start insulting each other.

Here's what some of the kids said to me:

- Tyler: "*Thou greasy, evil-eyed minimus!*"
- Ashley: "*Thou reeky, raw-boned ruffian!*"
- Kayla: "*Thou jaded, hunch-backed nut-hook!*"
- Ayesha: "*Thou saucy, sour-faced dogfish!*"
- Zack: "*Thou yeasty, fat-kidneyed cutpurse!*"

Everyone was laughing and having a great time, and for a minute I forgot about Peter. Then I saw him across the room and realized he was having just as much fun as the rest of us. I guess, since these were all words Shakespeare had used, Peter was able to say them. He made his way over to me, and after I said my line to him, he shouted, "*Thou brazen, shag-eared rabbit-sucker!*"

It took Ms. Hastings a while to get us all to settle down again, but then she asked us what we thought about what we'd done. The class pretty much agreed it was fun and we wanted to do more stuff like this. I looked over at Peter, who was dying to say something. I put my finger over my lips to tell him not to, but before I knew it, he shouted out, "*O wonderful, wonderful, and most wonderful! and yet again wonderful.*" And of course everyone laughed at him.

When everyone had calmed down, Ms. Hastings handed a three-by-five-inch index card to each of us and said that each card contained a different line from a Shakespeare play. Our job was to pair up with someone in class and make a scene with just the words on the cards. We would then act them out in front of the class. She held up a big dictionary we could use if we needed to look up any words. There were a lot of questions following that, but instead of answering them she said, "Just do it!"

I got up and walked straight over to Peter, knowing no one else would be able to communicate with him. And since most of the other kids thought he was strange, I didn't have any competition to work with him. Everyone seemed to be into this, and Ms. Hastings moved around the room encouraging us.

"Let me see your card," I said to Peter. "Mine says, '*O, I am slain!*'"

He handed me his card, which read, "*She should have died hereafter.*"

"Let's figure out how to act this out. I'm telling you that I'm dying, but I'm not sure what yours means." I went to the front of the room and looked up *hereafter* in the dictionary. There were quite a few definitions, but I guessed that on Peter's card it meant "at a time in the future." I walked back over to Peter and told him the definition. "So, you're saying that it would have been better if I died later. How about I run over to you, grab your hand, say my line, and then die? Then you look at me and say yours?"

"*Yes, yes; the lines are very quaintly writ,*" he said.

"Whatever. So, let's try it out."

We rehearsed our scene, and Peter asked, "*Shall this our lofty scene be acted over?*" So we went through it once more to be sure.

After about five minutes of rehearsing, Ms. Hastings told the class to take our seats, and when we were ready we should come to the front and present our scenes. "While a pair is acting out a scene, the rest of you need to pay attention and applaud wildly when it's over."

Jayden and Emily went first. Jayden sat in a chair. Emily slowly walked over to him and said, "*Let me be your servant: though I look old, yet I am strong and lusty.*"

Jayden looked Emily over and said, "*Get thee to a nunnery.*" The class roared with laughter, and the two of them took their bows.

Tiffany and Jasmine went next. They pretended to be fighting, and Jasmine put her hand around Tiffany's neck. Tiffany said, "*I prithee, take thy fingers from my throat.*"

Jasmine replied, "*My soul is too much charged with blood of thine already.*" We applauded again.

Then Tyler and Rose performed. Tyler reached for Rose's hand and said, "*Do not you love me?*"

We all laughed when Rose pushed him away and said, "*Get you gone, you minimus.*"

After a few more kids acted out their scenes, I motioned to Peter that it was our turn. My death scene was fabulous. I grabbed my chest, went down on one knee, and said my line: "*O, I am slain.*" Then I fell on my back and just lay there.

Peter took a deep breath, looked at me on the floor, and said, "*She should have died hereafter.*" I was ready to get up and take a bow, but when I looked at Peter, I saw he wasn't finished. He looked out at the class and began again:

> *She should have died hereafter;*
> *There would have been a time for such a word.*
> *To-morrow, and to-morrow, and to-morrow,*
> *Creeps in this petty pace from day to day*
> *To the last syllable of recorded time,*
> *And all our yesterdays have lighted fools*
> *The way to dusty death. Out, out, brief candle!*
> *Life's but a walking shadow, a poor player*
> *That struts and frets his hour upon the stage*

And then is heard no more: it is a tale
Told by an idiot, full of sound and fury,
Signifying nothing.

What followed was incredible silence. From my position on the floor, I could see the stunned class and, in the back of the room, an even more stunned Ms. Hastings. Finally, she broke the silence by clapping loudly, and the rest of the class joined her. I quickly got up, stood next to Peter, and took a bow. But they weren't applauding for me; Peter was the star now.

The rest of the kids did their scenes, and as soon as the bell rang, Peter and I darted out of the classroom. We didn't want to discuss with Ms. Hastings what had happened. At least not now. As we pushed past a crowd of kids by their lockers, Peter said to me, "*I do believe that these applauses are for some new honors.*"

After school, Peter and I met his parents outside the main office and told the secretary we had an appointment with Dr. Duncan, the principal. She sent us down the hall to where Dr. Duncan's door was sitting open. When we walked in, we were shocked to see Ms. Hastings and the guidance counselor Mr. Donnelly sitting next to the principal.

Before I could stop him, Peter walked over to Dr. Duncan and said, "*Madam, good even to your ladyship.*" She gave him a stern scowl, but then everyone sat down and Mrs. Marlowe changed the subject by asking Dr. Duncan if it was all right for me to be there. Mrs. Marlowe explained I would be able to help Peter communicate. Dr. Duncan looked confused but said she would allow it.

Then Mr. Marlowe told them the whole story of what had happened to Peter the week before and how he really couldn't help what he was doing. The principal, the guidance counselor, and Ms. Hastings kept looking at each other and then looking at Peter. It was pretty clear they didn't believe what they were hearing.

After Mr. Marlowe finished his explanation, Dr. Duncan looked over to Ms. Hastings and said, "Will you please tell everyone about the stunt Peter pulled in your class today?"

"Well, I'm not sure it was a stunt, but he must have memorized a long speech from *Macbeth* and showed up the rest of the class by performing it during an activity. I like initiative, but he was just showing off."

Suddenly, my phone buzzed. I looked down at a text from Peter: tell them i can't help it. i'm not trying 2 show off. i just open my mouth n all those words come out.

I translated. "Excuse me," I interrupted. "Peter wants me to tell you he can't help it. He says he's not trying to show off, but he just opens his mouth and all those lines come out. He can text me stuff in normal English...sort of."

Another text: i'm sorry n i'll try to control myself. tell ms. h i wasn't trying 2 show off. i didn't even know where that scene came from.

"He says he's sorry and really wants to apologize to Ms. Hastings," I said, turning to her. "He didn't even know where the scene was from."

"Tell him we're trying to understand this, but he's making it very difficult," Dr. Duncan said. "Tell him we're trying to help."

"You can tell him yourself. He can understand English," I said. "He just can't speak normally."

"Sorry," said Dr. Duncan, turning to Peter. "Peter, I want you to talk to the school psychologist, Dr. Goldstein. I'll make an appointment for you to see him tomorrow."

"Actually, we were thinking of taking him to see a psychologist anyway," said Mrs. Marlowe. "But if you want to have Dr. Goldstein talk to him instead, that's fine with us. We just want him to get over this. And could Emma go to the meeting with Dr. Goldstein? She really helps Peter communicate."

"That's fine," Dr. Duncan said abruptly. "In the meantime, I'll ask Mr. Donnelly to notify all Peter's teachers that he can't speak in class, and they shouldn't call on him. Is that all right, Peter?" It was pretty clear she was uncomfortable with Peter's condition and wanted this meeting to end as soon as possible.

"*Things that, to hear them told, have made me tremble; I will do it without fear or doubt,*" he said.

And with that, everyone got up and shook hands for no apparent reason. As we were leaving, Peter blurted out, "*Farewell! God knows when we shall meet again.*"

CHAPTER EIGHT

"FULL OF SCORPIONS IS MY MIND"

The next day, Peter wasn't at the bus stop, so I figured his mom or dad must've driven him to school. I got a note in homeroom from Mr. Donnelly telling me to be in Dr. Goldstein's office at the start of first period. I had only met Dr. Goldstein once, when he came to our class to talk about bullying. If someone asked me to draw a picture of a psychologist, it would look like him. He had a gray beard, a worn, brown jacket with those suede patches on the elbows, and a calm look about him. I remember he showed us this video about some kid who was bullied by kids in his school and then killed himself. It was a dumb video, and I think all of us were tired of being warned about the evils of bullying. We heard about bullying in every grade, and it didn't seem to help at all. Kids still could be mean to each other.

When I got to Dr. Goldstein's office, Peter and his mom were already waiting outside. Peter said to me, "*Good morrow, gentle lady.*" I just smiled back at him.

The door opened, and Dr. Goldstein asked us all to come in. "Call me Dr. G," he said, sitting down.

The office had several chairs and an old, ratty couch. I'd heard he usually led group sessions with a bunch of kids at the same time, but Peter and I were the only kids in this session. When we all sat down, Mrs. Marlowe told Dr. Goldstein I was there to help translate Peter's words. He seemed reluctant but agreed. He looked right at Peter and said: "So how do you feel today, Peter? I understand you've been acting a bit differently."

"*Full of scorpions is my mind!*" Peter shouted.

"I'm sorry to hear that, Peter," Dr. Goldstein said. "What can I do for you?

Peter started to shake. "*Is there no way to cure this? No new device to beat this from my brains?*"

We all froze. Mrs. Marlowe grabbed Peter's hand and tried to calm him down. He pulled away from her, pulled out his cell phone, and started to tap away.

My phone buzzed, and I read the text aloud: "I don't feel good because I'm still speaking like Shakespeare. What can you do to help me? I can't take it anymore."

"Tell him I'll do whatever I can," Dr. Goldstein said.

"You can tell him yourself, Dr. G. He can hear you."

"Of course. Sorry, Peter." He said, turning to Peter. "Do you *think* in Shakespeare's words as well?"

Peter texted like crazy, and I read it aloud again: "No, I think in normal words, but they all come out in Shakespeare's words. I'm thinking a sentence in plain English, but when I say it, it comes out funny."

Dr. Goldstein asked "Do you hear voices in your head? And if so, do they speak like Shakespeare?"

I continued reading Peter's responses. "No, I don't hear any voices. I'm not crazy, doc. I just have this speech problem. Is there a pill or something you can give me to stop it?"

"No, Peter," he said. "I can't give out pills because I'm not a psychiatrist. Only they can do that. But I don't think drugs will help you. I think you'll just have to concentrate more before you speak."

I looked down at the next text that came in: ur a jerk. i'm wasting my time with u! i wanna get out of here. I started to laugh but simply said, "Uh, Peter says 'Thanks, but I think it's time to go to class.'"

"Sure, sure," Dr. Goldstein said. "I'm sorry I couldn't help you any more."

It looked like he couldn't wait to get rid of Peter, just as Dr. Duncan had looked yesterday. It was clear no one understood or knew how to handle Peter's bizarre condition.

Mrs. Marlowe thanked me for coming and told Peter she'd see him after school.

Peter turned to Dr. Goldstein and said, "*Did you ever cure any so? Til then, adieu.*"

CHAPTER NINE

"IN MY HEAD AND IN MY HEART"

W hen I got to the bus stop Wednesday morning, Peter was already there. He looked really happy and was wearing a particularly wild Hawaiian shirt. This one was bright red with big white flowers. I asked him how he was, hoping he'd have a normal reply.

"I'll write it straight," he said. *"The matter's in my head and in my heart."* He then reached into his backpack and took out a whiteboard about the size of a notebook. He uncapped a dry erase marker and started writing furiously, and then held the board out for me to read:

> *I think I have a solution to my problem!*

"Really? What is it?" I asked.

He took out a small eraser from his backpack. He wiped the board clean and wrote:

> *This board!*

I let out a groan because I'd thought for a moment he'd actually figured out how to stop talking like Shakespeare. This didn't sound like much of a solution. But he erased the board and wrote:

> Now I can just write out my words and I can talk to my teachers that way.

I took the board from him and started to write out my next question. He grabbed it back and wrote:

> I can still hear you! We won't have to text back and forth anymore.

ERASE

I'm
sure my
teachers will
understand.

ERASE

My parents
talked to
the principal
again.

ERASE

> She and
> Mr. Donnelly
> told all my
> teachers
> about me.

ERASE

> And they
> told them
> about using
> the board.

As he was erasing the board to write something else, I interrupted and asked how he was going to explain his problem when kids asked him what was wrong. This seemed to stump him for a while. I guess he hadn't even thought about that, especially because kids usually avoided him. But I had a feeling seeing him toting around that board and hearing those Shakespeare lines slip out once in a while, some kids would be bothering him now. "Some of those kids might tease you," I said. "I heard a few kids complaining about you after English class. Max said he was going to get you."

"*For my part, I care not.*"

"Well, you should care. He's a big guy."

"*That shall be as it may.*"

"What if Max calls you out and starts a fight?"

"*I dare not fight; but I will wink and hold out mine iron.*"

"Your iron? What are you talking about?"

"*Zounds, I would make him eat a piece of my sword,*" he said.

"Peter, stop being stupid. First of all, you don't have a sword, and second, even if you did, you wouldn't use it. What are you going to say to Max if he threatens you?"

"*Then have at you with my wit! I will dry-beat you with an iron wit, and put up my iron dagger.*"

"Well I'm sure your wit will make him quake in his boots. Listen, you've got to have a plan for when kids start to bother you."

"*What would you have me do?*" he asked. He suddenly looked very worried.

"I don't know, but I'll think of something. Look, here comes the bus."

It dawned on me we'd just had an entire conversation, and I hadn't even realized he was quoting Shakespeare. I guess I was finally starting to get used to the language. "Let's talk after school. I'll see you in English class."

CHAPTER TEN

"THE TRAFFIC OF OUR STAGE"

W hen we got to English class that day, Ms. Hastings had some great activities planned for us. As soon as the bell rang, she said, "Today we're finally going to start reading *Romeo and Juliet.* We're going to take part of a scene, read it a few times, and then get it up on its feet."

"What does that mean?" someone shouted out.

"It means we're going to treat this scene just the way actors treat it. We're going to turn our classroom into a rehearsal studio. When actors start a play, the first thing they do is read it aloud a few times, and then they try acting it out. Rather than just read this play, we're going to perform it."

Suddenly my phone began to vibrate. I looked over at Peter and saw he was busy texting me more messages. When he looked up, I shook my head and made a motion for him to write it out. He smiled and pulled out his white board. He started to wave the board to get Ms. Hastings's attention, but she held up a hand to stop him and explained to the class what was going on. "As you may have heard, our friend Peter is, uh, having a problem speaking. So his teachers have agreed to let him use a white board to ask questions. Uh, but he will be able to speak Shakespeare's words, so he can participate in our scenes."

There was a loud buzz throughout the class. By then, most kids had heard him saying weird stuff in other classes, and of course he'd rattled off that whole speech from *Macbeth* in Ms. Hastings's class already. It took a bit for Ms. Hastings to quiet everyone down.

She had us move our desks into a circle and then passed out a piece of paper to each of us that read at the top:

Romeo and Juliet
Act 1
Prologue

Her instructions were to just read around the circle and stop reading at each end punctuation mark. Someone asked her what that meant, and she explained it was anything except a comma— so a period, semicolon, colon, question mark, or exclamation point counted.

Jenny was the first to read. She began:

Two households, both alike in dignity,
In fair Verona, where we lay our scene,
From ancient grudge break to new mutiny,
Where civil blood makes civil hands unclean.

Then Marcy read:

From forth the fatal loins of these two foes
A pair of star-cross'd lovers take their life;

Then I read:

Whose misadventured piteous overthrows
Do with their death bury their parents' strife.

Then Byron read:

The fearful passage of their death-mark'd love,
And the continuance of their parents' rage,
Which, but their children's end, nought could remove,
Is now the two hours' traffic of our stage;

Peter was next, and I held my breath, but all he did was say the next line:

The which if you with patient ears attend,
What here shall miss, our toil shall strive to mend.

Ms. Hastings said, "Please continue from the top." So we went on until we had heard it five times, and everyone had read once. Then, she asked us to stand up and had the boys move to the left side of the room and the girls move to the right side.

Everyone was trying to figure out what was going on. Usually Ms. Hastings would give us poems or stories to read and tell us what they were going to be about. Then we would read, and she would tell us what everything meant. But instead of telling us what it meant this time, she had the boys and the girls read the lines back and forth to one another in what she called a "choral reading." It sounded pretty cool once we did it out loud. And then she said, "Let's do it one more time, but say it louder and stay together."

I'm sure the teachers in the rooms next to ours must have been freaking out because we were shouting by the time we finished. And guess what? It sounded like a conversation between two groups of people—almost like an argument. It started to really make sense, and when she asked us some questions about it, it was pretty clear the guy speaking is talking about these two lovers, Romeo Montague and Juliet Capulet, whose parents hate each other and because of that, the lovers die. "And it only takes two hours," Max said. And we figured it all out without Ms. Hastings's telling us what it meant.

We sat back down in our circle, and she passed out another handout. We did another read-around, this time with the next part of the play. But she said she had shortened it a bit for us. Also, she explained that "1.1" was short for "Act 1 Scene 1," which is how Shakespeare's plays are broken up.

Romeo and Juliet, 1.1 edited
Enter Sampson and Gregory, of the house of Capulet, armed with swords and bucklers

Sampson: A dog of the house of Montague moves me.
Gregory: The quarrel is between our masters and us their men.
Sampson: 'Tis all one, I will show myself a tyrant.
Gregory: Draw thy tool! Here comes two of the house of the Montagues. I will frown as I pass by, and let them take it as they list.

Sampson: Nay. I will bite my thumb at them; which is a disgrace to them, if they bear it.

Enter two other Servingmen, Abraham and Balthasar

Abraham: Do you bite your thumb at us, sir?

Sampson: I do bite my thumb, sir.

Abraham: Do you bite your thumb at us, sir?

Sampson: *[Aside to Gregory]* Is the law of our side, if I say ay?

Gregory: No.

Sampson: No, sir, I do not bite my thumb at you, sir, but I bite my thumb, sir.

Enter Benvolio

Sampson: Draw if you be men. Gregory, remember thy washing blow.

They fight.

Benvolio: Part, fools! *[Drawing his sword]* Put up your swords.

Enter Tybalt [Drawing his sword]

Tybalt: Turn thee, Benvolio; look upon thy death.

Benvolio: I do but keep the peace. Put up thy sword, Or manage it to part these men with me.

Tybalt: What, drawn and talk of peace? I hate the word As I hate hell, all Montagues, and thee. Have at thee, coward! *[They fight]*

Enter three or four citizens with clubs or partisans

Citizens: Clubs, bills and partisans! Beat them down! Down with the Capulets! Down with the Montagues!

Enter old Capulet in his gown, and Lady Capulet

Capulet: What noise is this? Give me my long sword, ho!

Lady Capulet: A crutch, a crutch! Why call you for
    a sword?
Enter old Montague and his wife
Capulet: My sword, I say. Old Montague is come
    And flourishes his blade in spite of me.
Montague: Thou villain Capulet!—Hold me not; let me go.
Lady Montague: Thou shalt not stir one foot to seek
    a foe.
Enter Prince Escalus with his train
Prince: Rebellious subjects, enemies to peace,
    Profaners of this neighbor-stain'd steel,
    Will they not hear?—what ho! You men, you
    beasts,
    That quench the fire of your pernicious rage
    With purple fountains issuing from your veins:
    On pain of torture, from those bloody hands
    Throw your mistempered weapons to the ground,
    And hear the sentence of your moved prince.
    If you ever disturb our streets again
    Your lives shall pay the forfeit of the peace.

We read this scene in the circle, the way we had with the
Prologue, stopping at end punctuation marks. The first time
around, it didn't make any sense. Most of us struggled with the
words and read it in a boring tone. Except for Peter, of course. His
line—*Rebellious subjects, enemies to peace, / Profaners of this neigh-
bor-stain'd steel, / Will they not hear?*—was delivered loudly and
passionately, and everyone laughed. But Ms. Hastings just smiled.

After round one, she asked us if we knew what was going on,
and we all agreed we hadn't a clue. I saw Peter waving his board,

but Ms. Hastings gave him a gentle sign to wait before he explained it to the class. So we read it again, but this time she asked us to circle or highlight any words or phrases we didn't understand. And instead of stopping at the punctuation marks this time, she told us to just read an entire character's part and then switch readers.

The second time through it started to actually make a little sense, and several hands went up when we had finished and Ms. Hastings asked again what it meant. Again, I could see Peter looking frustrated that she was ignoring his waving board, but he seemed to be giving up because he wasn't the only one who'd figured out there's a street fight between the two families, the Capulets and the Montagues, and that the prince comes in and breaks it up.

When she asked us what words we didn't know, there were a lot—*partisans, washing blow, profaners, pernicious, mistempered*—but we sort of figured them out together. But three things struck all of us as funny.

"What does, '*Give me my long sword, ho,*' mean?" asked Jose. "Who's he calling a 'ho'?" When all the laughing stopped, Ms. Hastings said it was just an expression like "Yo" or "Hey."

Max then asked, "What's this thumb-biting stuff? Is that like giving someone the finger?"

"Actually, you're right, Max," Ms. Hastings said. "It's an old-fashioned insult, just like giving someone the finger."

"So maybe I'll start doing that and not get in trouble anymore," he said. With that he turned to Byron and bit his thumb at him. Byron laughed and did it back to Max. Before long everyone was biting thumbs and laughing like crazy. Even Ms. Hastings got into it but finally told us all to stop.

Then Audrey asked, "What does it mean when it says, '*Enter Prince Escalus with his train*'?"

Ms. Hastings laughed out loud. "I never thought of that, but it just means his people are following him, like an entourage. There were no trains in Shakespeare's lifetime. I guess it does sound kind of silly."

After we had read it three times, it really started to make a lot of sense. We discussed it further, and together we figured out these two families have been fighting long time, and two Capulets, Gregory and Sampson, are out walking and come across two Montague guys, Abraham and Balthasar (who doesn't say anything), and then they start to fight. Benvolio tries to break it up, but then Tybalt shows up, more people come, and there's a huge battle. Then the Prince comes and stops them. He tells them if he ever catches any members of the families fighting again, they'll be killed.

Ms. Hastings congratulated us for figuring all that out without her. Then she asked us a few questions about where we should stage this scene for our rendition. The suggestions were a dark alley, the main street in a town, the mall, and the schoolyard. We voted for the mall because that sounded like a fun place to do it. And I think we secretly thought we'd actually get to take a field trip to the mall to perform it.

She then said that we'd read it one more time, but this time she was going to have kids stand in the front of the room and play actual characters. She just gave out the parts at random. It was funny, some girls got to read the lines that were supposed to be boys' and some boys got to read the girls' lines (but there weren't too many girl parts.) I think there were about twelve parts, and I got to play the part of Benvolio. Peter didn't get a part, and when I looked over at him, he seemed angry. So I figured it best if I just ignored him.

I got a text: he's a good guy trying 2 stop every1 from fighting. he should sound like a nice guy.

I looked over at him and rolled my eyes. Apparently he thought he was the only one who could figure that out. When my turn came, I gave a great performance as Benvolio.

I couldn't believe it. It *really* made sense after we acted it out, and those of us who were reading it actually knew what we were saying. Some kids even started shaking their fists and yelling at each other. It was hysterical. Those who were just watching even clapped when we were done.

Ms. Hastings seemed thrilled—and maybe a bit relieved that it was working. She said, "You guys were great today! We're going to really get this scene up on its feet right here in class tomorrow." She said we'd volunteer for parts, and those of us in the last reading couldn't take a part the next time. All the kids in the other group raised their hands to volunteer, and the parts were quickly assigned. Peter got the part of Montague, and he seemed happy at that.

We all came to class the next day a little more excited than usual. English had always been my favorite subject, but what we were doing was totally new and kind of cool.

As soon as we got settled, Ms. Hastings told us we were going to stage and direct the scene. Then, so we could tell all the actors apart, she gave each of them one of those "HELLO, my name is..." stickers on which she had written the character's name. Peter proudly pasted his right on his Hawaiian shirt: "HELLO, my name is MONTAGUE."

Ms. Hastings explained that those of us without speaking parts were the directors and had to raise our hands if we had suggestions about the scene. She said the actors on stage couldn't give their opinions. They could only say their lines and do what we told them to do. We had to decide who came on stage first, second, and so on, and from what side each character would enter. That was pretty tricky, because the handout didn't really tell us any of that information. Eventually we made some decisions that seemed right, and we were ready to go.

Before we got started, Ms. Hastings pulled out some toy Nerf swords from the closet and handed them out to the actors.

Soon the scene was going strong; our directions and the actors were great. When it came to Peter's lines, he fit right in and didn't try to show off or anything. Just as the prince was saying his last lines, the bell rang. I couldn't believe class was over. We'd had such a good time, and we really got that scene.

As I made my way out the door, Peter came over to me and said, "*Our revels now are ended. These our actors, as I foretold you, were all spirits and are melted into air, into thin air.*"

A bunch of kids heard him and started to laugh.

"So, Peter can only talk like Shakespeare?" Max asked me.

"Is he for real?" added Byron.

I didn't want to say anything and wasn't sure how to react. But Peter actually chimed in and said, "*You are right, courteous knights.*" And with that they started laughing and ran down the hall.

CHAPTER ELEVEN

"TWO BLUSHING PILGRIMS"

T he class continued to work on *Romeo and Juliet* for the rest of that week and all of the next through a series of fun activities. One day, Ms. Hastings showed us three movie versions of the balcony scene (you know, the famous "O *Romeo, Romeo! wherefore art thou Romeo?*" scene). Most of the class liked the Baz Luhrmann version best, probably because they used guns instead of swords and drove some fancy cars. I guess I'm a romantic because I liked the traditional version from 1968.

One day just after we started Act 5, Ms. Hastings told us we were going to perform a shortened version of the play for the whole school. Some of the kids groaned, but some of us were excited. Of course, Peter and I were thrilled.

The following Friday, Ms. Hastings assigned us our parts. Believe it or not, Peter was cast as Romeo, and I was cast as Juliet. I was sort of shocked she picked us, but Peter simply said, "*I'll perform to the last article.*" I told Peter we should get together over the weekend to begin rehearsing. He agreed, adding, *"We must needs dine together."*

I showed up at Peter's house that evening for pizza and our first rehearsal. He answered the door and bowed, saying, *"A hundred thousand welcomes!"* The guy from O Sole Mio's Pizza had already made his delivery, and the family was about to sit down to eat. Peter's parents greeted me and let me know they were so glad I could join them. Of course, Peter more dramatically said, *"Sit down and welcome to our table."*

The conversation at dinner was mostly polite chatter. Peter's parents asked a lot of questions about what we were doing with *Romeo and Juliet* in school. I think they were secretly thrilled to have a simple conversation that didn't include a series of Shakespeare lines as replies.

After dinner, Peter and I started working on our parts in the family room. It turned out he had a bunch of scenes without me in them, and I had a bunch without him, so we just focused on the ones we had together.

We started with Romeo and Juliet's first meeting in Act 1, scene 5, when they instantly fall in love during a party at Juliet's house. Ms. Hastings had called it the "palmers scene" because Romeo and Juliet touch the palms of their hands together.

Here's the scene:

Romeo: *[To Juliet]* If I profane with my unworthiest hand
This holy shrine, the gentle fine is this:
My lips, two blushing pilgrims, ready stand
To smooth that rough touch with a tender kiss.

Juliet: Good pilgrim, you do wrong your hand too much,
Which mannerly devotion shows in this;
For saints have hands that pilgrims' hands do touch,
And palm to palm is holy palmers' kiss.

Romeo: Have not saints lips, and holy palmers too?

Juliet: Ay, pilgrim, lips that they must use in prayer.

Romeo: O, then, dear saint, let lips do what hands do;
They pray, grant thou, lest faith turn to despair.

Juliet: Saints do not move, though grant for prayers' sake.

Romeo: Then move not, while my prayer's effect I take.
Thus from my lips, by yours, my sin is purged.

Juliet: Then have my lips the sin that they have took.

Romeo: Sin from thy lips? O trespass sweetly urged!
Give me my sin again.

Juliet: You kiss by the book.

We worked on the scene for about a half hour, trying to figure out what was going on and what we should be doing during each line. Peter finally looked up "Romeo and Juliet 1.5" on YouTube and found a ton of videos of the scene. There was an old 1968-movie version, a 1996-movie version, some animated versions some kids had made, and even one done with LEGOs. And they were all completely different. The one thing that was the same in all of them was Romeo and Juliet kissed at the end.

We had a problem.

On Monday I asked Ms. Hastings for some help with the scene. She said the first fourteen lines form a perfect sonnet, which is a fourteen-line poem with ten syllables in each line. She said Shakespeare's sonnets always follow an ABAB CDCD EFEF GG rhyme scheme. So the palmers scene rhymes like this:

A: hand
B: this
A: stand
B: kiss
C: much
D: this
C: touch
D: kiss
E: too
F: prayer
E: do
F: despair
G: sake
G: take

She explained that a sonnet is a love poem. "It's important that, when these two strangers meet, the first thing that they do is make a sonnet together," she said. "That's what I call love. And they don't even realize they're making a work of art. And notice in the last line Juliet actually finishes Romeo's sentence."

I counted the lines and saw what she was saying, but the scene—and the rhyming—went on after the sonnet was over. So the next lines ended in:

H: purged
I: took
H: urged
I: book

"What's going on when Romeo says the next line, '*Thus from my lips, by yours, my sin is purged?*'" I asked. "It's the fifteenth line."

"If you look at the next few lines, you can see the lovers have started a new sonnet," she said. "Those are the first four lines of the new sonnet."

"But why don't they finish it?" I asked.

"Aha!" she exclaimed. "The nurse interrupts them and stops the sonnet. She represents the adult world. We'll see later that the adults cause all the problems for these two."

There was one other question I had to ask her, and I was sort of afraid of her answer. "Um, that line about the kiss, does it mean they really kiss each other? And I guess what I'm asking is, do Peter and I really have to kiss each other?"

She smiled, put her arm on my shoulder, and said, "Well, Emma, I guess I can't actually make you kiss Peter. But that's how the scene's written. I'll tell you what, why don't you just do 'air kisses' during rehearsal, and you two can decide whether or not you want to make it a real kiss for the school performance?"

Somehow I'd known the answer before I asked the question, but it was even scarier hearing it from her. As you might recall, I still had never kissed a boy at that point. Now I probably would have to do it in front of the whole school.

CHAPTER TWELVE

"'TIS TRUE: THERE'S MAGIC IN THE WEB"

N ow let me tell you how Peter really became famous. It turns out a kid in our class, Sarah Ansler, had mentioned Peter's new ability to her parents. Mrs. Ansler just happened to be an editor for *Newsday*, the Long Island newspaper. So a reporter from *Newsday* called Peter's parents and explained they wanted to do an article about him. His parents later told me they weren't sure it was a good idea, but Peter had convinced them to let the reporter come over and interview them.

I found out about the article the following Monday morning when I came down for breakfast, and my dad was reading the paper like he always did. But that morning, he handed it to me and said, "Check out your friend in the paper."

On page five was a picture of Peter followed by the article:

Local Boy Speaks Only Shakespeare

By Eric York

Long Island, N.Y.—Shakespeare has been dead for over 400 years, but a 12-year-old Long Island boy, Peter Marlowe, has an unusual problem that is keeping The Bard of Avon alive: he can only speak the playwright's lines.

According to his mother, Joan Marlowe, it all started when Peter, an eighth-grade student at Edward King Middle School, suffered a concussion after a heavy book of Shakespeare's works fell on the boy's head. "He was a pretty normal kid until a few weeks ago," she says. "And then he started speaking this way. We thought he was faking it at first, but now we're convinced he's not."

When asked about his condition, Peter insists this is no joking matter: "Sir, understand you this of me in sooth: Verily, I do not jest with you." His answer is a combination of lines from two of Shakespeare's plays: *The Taming of the Shrew* and *Coriolanus*.

Peter, whose hobbies include baseball and collecting, is able to communicate through normal language only by texting or by writing down what he wants to say. But, he says, Shakespeare's words are the only thing he can say out loud.

The school and Peter's teachers have been cooperating with him, according to a district spokesperson. And coincidentally, his English class is now studying *Romeo and Juliet*. Ellen Hastings, Peter's English teacher, explains that classmates have accepted Peter's condition. "At first they all thought he was acting out a scene from the play," she says. "But once they realized he couldn't help himself, they kind of just got used to it."

Peter says he is happy the class is reading Shakespeare now, and he looks forward to being in school each day. "Here I am to speak what I do know," he quotes from *Julius Caesar.* "I have neither wit, nor words to stir men's blood: I only speak right on."

It looks like "all the world's a stage" at Edward King Middle School thanks to Peter Marlowe.

Lots of kids must've seen the article because when Peter and I got on the bus that day, some of them cheered for him. He waved at them all and said, *"Thanks to all at once and to each one."* At that, they all clapped and someone in the back yelled, "More!" Everyone on the bus began chanting, "More! More!" That was all Peter needed. So as the bus drove us all to school, Peter gave a speech to everyone onboard:

> *Friends, Romans, countrymen, lend me your ears;*
> *I come to bury Caesar, not to praise him.*
> *The evil that men do lives after them;*
> *The good is oft interred with their bones...*

The speech lasted for most of the ride, but when Peter finished with *"Brutus was an honorable man,"* the kids applauded like crazy and started pounding on the seats and stomping on the floor for an encore. So Peter started another speech: *"Once more unto the breach..."* But the bus driver had had enough and slammed on the brakes. She looked in the mirror and said if Peter didn't stop, she'd report them all to the principal. The bus was silent the rest of the way to school.

When we walked into school, some kids Peter didn't even know gave him high fives and called out to him things like, "Hey, way to go Peter!" He was so thrilled to be getting so much attention he completely forgot I was with him. That really hurt, but I tried to be happy for him.

CHAPTER THIRTEEN

"I DO NOT JEST"

Once the word spread that day that Peter could quote Shakespeare anytime and anyplace, kids started testing him. It didn't seem to bother him too much. Once, as we were walking to class, someone yelled out to him, "Hey, say something in Shakespeare!"

Peter was quick to reply, *"Peace, you mumbling fool!"*

There were lots of incidents like that all day, but the real craziness began that afternoon when we had a substitute in English. It was Mrs. Minola, who we all knew because she had been doing substitute work forever. She looked like she was at least a hundred years old.

"Ms. Hastings is at a teachers' conference today, and the department chair told me to have you do this work," she said, holding up a worksheet. "He said it would be a good review of the play you're reading." She passed out the worksheet on *Romeo and Juliet* and said we were allowed to use our books.

I looked down at the questions and read the first ten:

Romeo and Juliet Review Questions
1. What is the setting for the play?
2. Who is fighting at the beginning of the first scene?
3. Which character tries to stop the fighting among the servants in Act 1?
4. Which character is aggressive and eager to fight in Act 1?
5. What threat does the Prince make to Lord Montague and Lord Capulet in the first scene?
6. Who has asked for Juliet's hand in marriage?
7. How old is Juliet?
8. Why is Romeo so sad?
9. What is Benvolio's advice to Romeo?
10. Explain how Romeo finds out about the Capulet ball.

As we looked it over, the whole class moaned at the same time. We had already read a lot of the play, and we were eager to finish it. The handout was a big joke, just busy work to keep us quiet. Mrs. Minola tried to settle us down, but I could tell even she thought the worksheet was lame. So Jack raised his hand and asked her, "Mrs. Minola, can we let Peter say some of his Shakespeare lines to us? He has all of Shakespeare memorized, and it's really cool."

"I doubt he has *all* of Shakespeare memorized," Mrs. Minola said.

"No, really, he does," said Megan. "Let him show you."

"Well, Peter. Is this right?" Mrs. Minola asked.

"*Ay, Madam,*" Peter said, "*'Tis in my memory lock'd.*"

"If that's true, Peter," she said, "let me hear you recite Sonnet 18 for us."

For a moment, I was worried for Peter. I hadn't heard him quote anything other than Shakespeare's plays so far. He stood up and went to the front of the class. The class was cheering before he even began speaking. Then he cleared his throat, the cheering quieted, and Peter began:

> *Shall I compare thee to a summer's day?*
> *Thou art more lovely and more temperate:*
> *Rough winds do shake the darling buds of May,*
> *And summer's lease hath all too short a date:*
> *Sometime too hot the eye of heaven shines,*
> *And often is his gold complexion dimm'd;*
> *And every fair from fair sometime declines,*
> *By chance or nature's changing course untrimm'd;*
> *But thy eternal summer shall not fade*
> *Nor lose possession of that fair thou owest;*
> *Nor shall Death brag thou wander'st in his shade,*
> *When in eternal lines to time thou growest:*
> *So long as men can breathe or eyes can see,*
> *So long lives this and this gives life to thee.*

The class erupted in applause, and Peter took a deep bow. I couldn't believe he knew the sonnets, too! He was having fun, and the kids all seemed to be on his side. Mrs. Minola looked like she didn't know what to say, but she clapped, too.

Rebecca said to Peter, "How about we just yell out a word and you give us a Shakespeare line with that word? Can you do that?"

"*Yes, without all doubt,*" said Peter.

"Wait a minute," said Mrs. Minola. "Let's do this in an organized way. We'll see if we can stump Peter. Everyone take out a piece of paper and write any word on it. You can pass them up, and I'll call them out to him. But make sure they're *clean* words."

That's how all the excitement began. We all got busy writing our words and passing them up front. We were all laughing and starting to get loud, but Mrs. Minola got us to settle down. She looked through the words, making nasty faces at some that were probably jokes.

She read off the first one: "Football."

Peter answered, "*Am I so round with you as you with me, that like a football you do spurn me thus?*"

Then she said, "Dog."

He responded, "*The cat will mew and dog will have his day.*"

"Horse," she said.

"*A horse! A horse! My kingdom for a horse!*"

"Apple."

"*Faith, as you say, there's small choice in rotten apples.*"

"Orange."

"*Give not this rotten orange to your friend.*"

"Dumb."

"*I have words to speak in thine ear will make thee dumb.*"

"Flower."

"*I am bound to you, that you on my behalf would pluck a flower.*"

"Bite."

"*Teeth hadst thou in thy head when thou wast born, to signify thou camest to bite the world.*"

"Strawberry."

"*The strawberry grows underneath the nettle and wholesome berries thrive and ripen best neighbour'd by fruit of baser quality.*"

"Stupid."

The class laughed at that one, but Peter didn't skip a beat. "*Pray you once more,*" he said, "*is not your father grown incapable of reasonable affairs? Is he not stupid?*"

"Shoes."

"*You have dancing shoes with nimble soles.*"

"Cheese."

"*His breath stinks with eating toasted cheese.*" Again, there was laughter.

But Mrs. Minola kept going. "Lucky," she said.

"*'Tis a lucky day, boy, and we'll do good deeds on it.*"

"Music."

"*If music be the food of love, play on.*"

"Shirt."

"*The naked truth of it is, I have no shirt.*"

Mrs. Minola made a face as she looked at the next piece of paper and started to lay it down, but then she grinned and called out "Ass!" The class erupted in laughter and cheers.

When everyone had quieted, Peter responded, "*Away! You are an ass, you are an ass.*" More cheers.

"Sick," Mrs. Minola said.

"*Pray, be not sick, for you must be our housewife.*"

"Christmas."

"*At Christmas I no more desire a rose than wish a snow in May's new-fangled mirth.*"

"Happy."

"*Go, girl, seek happy nights to happy days.*"

"School."

"*She was a vixen when she went to school; and though she be but little, she is fierce.*"

He was able to find a line for almost every word we came up with. And when he couldn't, he had a line for an answer. When Mrs. Minola presented him with "peanut butter," Peter responded, "*I have no words: My voice is in my sword: thou bloodier villain than terms can give thee out!*"

"Television," she continued.

"*No words, no words: hush.*"

"iPad?"

"*Pray you, let's have no words of this.*"

"All right, class," said Mrs. Minola. "That's all of the words. Peter, you were wonderful, and class we all should give him a hand." The applause lasted for a long time, and of course, Peter took many big bows before returning to his seat.

The bell rang a few minutes later, and everyone spilled out into the hall still buzzing with excitement. Bobby Kaplan ran up to Peter and me. "Hey, dude," he said to Peter, "I got the whole thing on video, and I just uploaded it to YouTube."

"Really?" I said. "That's so cool."

"Yeah," he responded. "It's called 'That Shakespeare Kid.' Check it out when you get home."

And that's how Peter got the nickname and how he (and I) became famous.

As soon as I got home, I watched Bobby's video on YouTube. It already had 453 hits at three thirty. At five o'clock when I checked again it had 1,254 hits. I sent Peter a text message about it, and he responded that he was following it, too. After dinner, the count was up to 6,517, and there were lots of funny comments about it. At eight o'clock it was up to 12,026. It was going viral!

Peter texted me around eight thirty.

Peter: did u c the utube hits? do u believe it?

Emma: YES! amazing!

Peter: i love it. it got 15,280 hits already.

Emma: u r famous!

Peter: yup. how cool is that?

By Wednesday, the YouTube video had gone completely viral and was up to over a million hits. It had really caught everyone's attention. Television stations started contacting the Marlowes to request interviews. Mr. and Mrs. Marlowe turned down most of the offers because it all was too crazy, but when the producer from *The Today Show* called, they agreed to go on.

Then something happened I really never expected. The producer asked them to take me along to join Peter for the interview! My parents were also invited, and NBC would be sending a limousine for all of us to go to the show. I couldn't believe it.

The *Today Show* interview was set for Friday, so the rest of the week dragged by. Peter and I chatted on IM at night, and he was so excited about his big moment on TV. He told me he was proud of what he could do, and he wanted to share it with as many people as possible. Every time he mentioned how many people would be watching, I grew more and more scared. He even Googled some information about the show and told me that over five million people watch it every morning. Then he pointed out that even more people would be able to see it when NBC put it up on their website after the live airing.

CHAPTER FOURTEEN

"PERCHANCE YOU WONDER AT THIS SHOW"

Friday morning finally rolled around, and my parents and I got up at about four thirty to be sure we were ready for the big day. Mrs. Marlowe said that when Peter awoke that morning, the first thing he said was, "*But, soft! What day is this?*"

At five thirty, an NBC limousine arrived at my house, and my parents and I climbed in. The Marlowes were already inside; of course Peter was wearing one of his Hawaiian shirts. I had put on the best dress I owned, so I couldn't help but laugh and roll my eyes at his choice of attire.

"I tried to get him to wear a suit," Mrs. Marlowe said, laughing with me, "but you know Peter and his shirts."

Peter gave a half smile and responded, "*Good day at once,*" ignoring our mocking of his shirt. "*A glooming peace this morning with it brings.*"

I wasn't sure what he meant by that. "Are you nervous?" I asked.

"*I have a faint cold fear thrills through my veins,*" he said. "*Fear comes upon me: O, much I fear some ill unlucky thing.*"

Usually he was the one trying to calm me down, but this time it was my turn to help him to relax. "It'll be great," I said. "And think, you'll really be famous after today. Everyone will know who you are. Did you sleep OK?"

"*I have not slept one wink,*" he said. "*I would give all my fame for a pot of ale and safety.*" At that, our parents all had a good laugh.

"OK, so now you're just saying stupid stuff," I said, laughing. "Knock it off."

After that, we were all pretty quiet for the forty-five-minute ride into the city. Not too many cars were on the road at that hour, and we eased through the Midtown Tunnel and drove right past the Empire State Building. As we approached NBC's headquarters at Thirty Rockefeller Plaza, the car became totally silent.

When we arrived, there were thousands of people waiting outside. I wondered for a moment if the crowd was there to see us, and then I remembered the latest winner from *American Idol* was going to be giving a concert in the Plaza. "Oh, yeah," I said. "They're all here to see that guy, Billy Burbage."

"*By'r lady, he is a good musician,*" said Peter.

"Well, maybe we'll get to meet him backstage in the greenroom," I said. "Wouldn't that be cool?"

"*Ay, forsooth.*"

The driver continued past the crowd and to back entrance of the building. We exited the car, and a security guard led us through the door to his desk. I was so excited I was actually shaking. A young man who introduced himself as one of the assistant producers met us at the security desk. "I'm thrilled to finally meet you, Peter," he said, extending his hand.

Peter was looking a little less nervous by then. He shook the man's hand and responded, *"Fair thoughts and happy hours attend on you!"*

The producer laughed and said, "That was great. This is going to be fun!" I got the idea he thought Peter was faking it. I'd seen that look many times before. Most everyone who met Peter during his Shakespeare days thought he was faking it.

The producer took us on the elevator up to the third floor, where the makeup department was. My mother had just started to let me wear makeup, but I only did it once in a while. And now a professional was making me up. I was so excited.

Peter looked uncomfortable sitting in the makeup chair next to mine. He looked over at me and said, annoyed, *"Frailty, thy name is woman."* Apparently he didn't approve of my fancy new look.

"Oh, give me a break, Peter," I said. "We ladies like to look good, especially on television."

"Well enough," he said. *"God has given you one face, and you make yourselves another."*

Before I could argue back, Al Roker actually walked into the room with a big smile on his face. *Oh my God*, I thought. *This is really happening. I can't believe it.* Al introduced himself to our parents first. As if they—and everyone else in the world—didn't know who he was. And then he came over to Peter and me. He shook my hand and introduced himself, but then he turned to Peter and said, "Forsooth. Art thou young Peter, that knavish lad that is calleth 'That Shakespeare Kid?' Prithee, if it be so, I want to shaketh thy hand." His impression of Shakespeare was way off.

"*Good morrow, noble sir,*" responded Peter, shaking Al's hand.

"They tell me you can only speak lines from Shakespeare. Are you just foolin' with us, or is it true?" he asked.

"*Ay,*" Peter replied, "*'tis true: 'tis true 'tis pity; and pity 'tis 'tis true.*"

"He means he's sorry he's doing it, but he can't help himself," I translated.

"Right," said Al. "Well, you guys are on in about thirty minutes. Break a leg."

"*Farewell, good fellow,*" said Peter. "*I'll talk with you more anon.*"

We were just finishing up our makeup when a producer came in with a clipboard in her hand and wearing a headset. "OK, I'm on it," she said into her microphone, smiling at us. "I'm bringing them down to the greenroom now." She then introduced herself as Lauren and led us back to the elevator.

We got out on the ground floor, and she walked us to the door of the greenroom. "You can wait in the visitors' lounge," she said to our parents, pointing toward a door just down the hall. Turning to Peter and me, she added, "You two head in here, and I'll be right back to prep you for the interview."

Our parents hugged us and wished us well. My mom and dad told me they were proud I was doing this. I tried to act cool and not show that I was nervous. Of course, Peter had to have the last word. "*Farewell, dear father! Adieu, my mother.*" Then we were alone.

Peter and I made our way into the greenroom. Here's what I noticed:

1. It wasn't green. It didn't even have a green plastic plant in it.
2. There were three giant TVs on the wall. One had a sign that said "Live" under it, and the others had signs that said "Camera 1" and "Camera 2."
3. Our new friend Al was doing the weather on the "Live" TV.
4. The couches were really comfortable.
5. There was lots of food and drinks on the table.
6. None of this seemed to calm my nerves, not even the food spread.

"I'm really nervous, Peter," I said. "I can't wait for this to be over."

"*Well, that fault may be mended with a breakfast,*" he said.

"Are you kidding? How can you eat at a time like this?"

"*They are never curst but when they are hungry,*" he said as he bit into a bagel and grabbed a bottle of orange juice.

Just then the door opened and the producer came in with none other than Billy Burbage. He was wearing this wild outfit with lots of glitter on it.

"This is Billy Burbage," she said to Peter. "He heard you were on the show and wanted to meet you."

"*Let me shake thy hand,*" said Peter, as Billy walked up to him.

"Sure thing, man," he said. "You know I really liked Shakespeare when I was in high school. He really knew how to write, man."

"*His very genius hath taken the infection of the device, man,*" Peter answered.

"Uh, sure. Whatever," Billy said. He took a bottle of water from the table and said, "Break a leg, you guys."

I really liked him and wanted to ask him for his autograph, but it was too late. He left as quickly as he had come in. Lauren went over a few things with us then. She said Matt Lauer would be interviewing us because he was a bit of a Shakespeare buff. He would be talking mostly to Peter, who would answer the questions in his (Shakespeare's) voice. But then Matt would explain who I was and that Peter and I were able to communicate by texting. Then he would ask Peter a few questions, and Peter would text me his answers so I could read them aloud. And finally Matt would ask Peter to say something about the weather so they could cut to Al. The whole segment would take four minutes.

It was then that I really started to panic. I mean, how many people would be watching us? What if I froze on camera and couldn't speak? What if Peter came across looking like a complete jerk? After all, he was my best friend—and I was really starting to like him in that other way—and I didn't want people to be laughing at him. I took out my phone and sent him a quick text: ur going 2 b great.

He responded: thanks. ur the best friend a kid could have. ☺ He turned and smiled at me. Then he did something strange. He gave me a big, long hug. After a few seconds, he pulled away and looked at me kind of oddly. He had a smile on his face I had never seen before. I didn't know what to think, but it looked like he was starting to think of me in a different way, too.

A few minutes later, Lauren came back into the greenroom. "Five minutes," she said. "Let's head out to the studio." We nervously followed her back to the studio, and when we got there all I could think was the set looked so small compared to what it looks like on TV.

They were just finishing a segment with some chef making spare ribs, and the hosts were all eating and saying how great it tasted. Then Matt Lauer said, "When we come back, we'll meet a young man who can only speak like Shakespeare. Really! We'll be right back."

As the stagehands came out and moved all the kitchen stuff away, Matt came over, shook our hands, and assured us this was going to be fun and we should just relax and enjoy it. I guess he was trying to get Peter in the mood when he said, "*Be not afraid of greatness: some are born great, some achieve greatness and some have greatness thrust upon them.*"

Peter just smiled at him. I think he was as nervous as I was. Lauren led us over to the couch, and we sat down across from Matt. She pointed out which camera we should look at and reminded us not to look at ourselves in the monitors. After a little bit, we heard the director say, "We're on in ten," and then proceed to count down to one. The camera light went on, and our four minutes of fame began.

Here's exactly how the interview went:

> **Matt:** Welcome back. We have a first on *The Today Show.* I want you to meet young Peter Marlowe. He's a thirteen-year-old from Long Island, and what makes him special is that he suddenly found himself unable to speak any words except those written by William Shakespeare. With him is his friend Emma Malcolm who he

is able to communicate to in in normal English by texting. Welcome to you both.

Peter: *Fair thoughts and happy hours attend on you.*

Matt: So, Peter, tell us how it felt to suddenly find yourself only speaking Shakespeare's words.

Peter: *Methought 'tis very strange. I have had a dream, past the wit of man to say what dream it was.*

Matt: And how do your friends and classmates react to you?

Peter: *O, I am mock'd...to make the world to laugh at me.*

Matt: I see. And what about your parents? What did they think?

Peter: *Though this be madness, yet there is method in 't.*

Matt: Is there anything you'd like to say to your parents now?

Peter: *Pardon, good father! good my mother, pardon! Perchance you wonder at this show.*

Matt: What do the doctors say about this?

Peter: *The time is out of joint.*

Matt: Were you big fan of Shakespeare before all this happened?

Peter: *Nay. It was Greek to me.*

Matt: I see. They tell me this started a little over three weeks ago. How have you been getting by in school all this time?

Peter: *Thou know'st that we two went to school together. [Pointing to Emma]*

Matt: Right. OK, so now let me ask Emma a few questions. How long have you known Peter?

Emma: About three years. We live down the street from each other.

Matt: Tell us about the accident that started all this.

Emma: We were in his mom's study, and he was trying to get her copy of this huge Shakespeare book off the top shelf so we could read *Romeo and Juliet* for class. He slipped and fell, and the book hit him on the head. He was unconscious for a few minutes. It wasn't until the next day that I realized this Shakespeare thing had started.

Matt: So what did you think the next day when you heard him quoting Shakespeare?

Emma: Well, Peter likes to joke around, so when we met at the bus stop, I thought he was just kidding. But then he texted me and told me he couldn't help himself. He was really scared.

Matt: So, how have you been helping Peter in school?

Emma: Um, we're only together in English class, so in his other classes he uses one of those little dry erase boards to talk to his teachers. But in English he's allowed to text his questions and comments to me. The teacher has been cool with that.

Matt: And are you reading Shakespeare in your English class now?

Emma: Yes, we're reading *Romeo and Juliet*, and we're going to perform a shortened version of it at school next week.

Matt: So, Peter can speak out loud in that class as long as he's sticking to the play?

Emma: Yes, and in our performance he's playing Romeo, and I'm playing Juliet.

Matt: Well, isn't that convenient? Are you practicing a lot?

Emma: Yes, but it's kind of not fair.

Matt: Why is that?

Emma: Because he has the whole play memorized, and I have to try to remember all my lines.

Matt: *[Laughing]* Yes, I can see how that would be a bit unfair. Now, Peter, let's try something out. I just happen to have a copy of *Romeo and Juliet* with me. How about I say a line, and then you try to finish it?

Emma: *[Reading a text from Peter]* Peter says this is going to be easy because he can recite the whole play.

Matt: Let's see if that's true. I'll start with a pretty famous passage: *Never was a story of more woe...*

Peter: *...than this of Juliet and her Romeo.*

Matt: That's perfect. Now, let's try a tougher one. Let me find it. *[Flipping through pages]* Ah, here it is: *What's in a name?*

Peter: *That which we call a rose by any other word would smell as sweet.*

Matt: Wow, that was amazing.

Emma: *[Reading a text from Peter.]* Peter says that that was easy. Do you want to ask him a tough one like a line from another one of Shakespeare's plays?

Matt: How about the opening line from *Twelfth Night*?

Peter: *If music be the food of love, play on.*

Matt: Young man, thou art a scholar. How about the first line of *Hamlet*?

Peter: *Who's there?*

Matt: Perfect again. How about the opening line from *Macbeth*?

Peter: *When shall we three meet again?*

Matt: I'm just amazed. OK, last one: what's the opening line of *Richard III*?

Peter: *Now is the winter of our discontent made glorious summer by this sun of York.*

Matt: Perfect. You're incredible, Peter. But I have one final question for you both. Is there any Romeo and Juliet romance going on between you two? You seem like you really care for each other.

I was stunned by the question. Sure, I'd been thinking Peter and I may have some feelings for each other, but this was on national TV, and I wasn't about to answer that question. I felt my throat go dry, and I looked at my phone to make sure I hadn't missed a text from Peter. But then he reached over and grabbed my hand, looked me in the eye, and said something I'll never forget.

Peter: *Plainly conceive, I love you.*
    I just froze and stared at the camera.
Matt: Wow. That sure answers that question. Let's hope your fate is better than the real Romeo and Juliet's. I want to thank you both for coming on, and I do hope your condition is only temporary, Peter. But before you go, can you introduce Al for his weather report?
Peter: *Fare thee well. [Looking to the right.] Prithee, who's there, besides foul weather?*
Al: 'Tis I, Al, the Man of the Weather. Thou speakest right, young lad.

As the camera light went out, Peter gave me a big hug, and Matt shook both of our hands. "You two were wonderful," he said. "Maybe we can have you back when you get your own voice back, Peter."

Lauren walked us back to the visitors' room where our parents were waiting. She thanked us all for coming and told us they'd be sending us DVD copies of the show. Then she gave us each a *Today Show* tote bag with lots of *Today Show* stuff in it, including a *Today Show* T-shirt, a *Today Show* hat, a *Today Show* mug, a *Today Show* mouse pad, a *Today Show* magnet, a *Today Show* pen, and a *Today Show* umbrella. Our parents told us they were proud of us, and my mom hugged me and started crying.

We left the building and walked to the limo, but I was still shaking. I couldn't get over what Peter had said to me. Was he just kidding, or did he really mean it? There was lots of talking on the way back to Long Island, but I didn't say very much.

The limo dropped Peter and me off at school because it was still pretty early in the day. Before we got out, we both put our fancy *Today Show* T-shirts on over our clothes (yes, even Peter covered up his Hawaiian shirt). English was about to start, so we quickly ran down the hall to the classroom.

When we walked in, something unbelievable happened. The whole class stood up and started clapping and cheering. Ms. Hastings came over and gave us both hugs, and most of the kids came over to us and gave us high fives. They told us the principal had shown our scene over the televisions in the classrooms to the *whole school*! Peter and I were thrilled with the way the kids greeted us, and at first I was excited everyone had watched our big debut. But then I realized the *whole school* had heard Peter say he loved me.

Ms. Hastings and the kids in the class asked us a ton of questions about *The Today Show* and Thirty Rockefeller Plaza. I decided to give Peter a break and answer most of them. After everyone settled down, Ms. Hastings told us we'd be rehearsing our scenes that day and would perform a thirty-minute version of the play the following week for the whole school. After the stunt Peter had pulled on *The Today Show* that morning, I was more nervous than ever about our onstage kiss.

CHAPTER FIFTEEN

"FOR GOODNESS' SAKE"

When Peter got home that afternoon, he had fifty-six voicemail messages on the family phone. Fifty-six! He and his parents didn't know what to do with all of them, so they just sat down and started listening to each one while Mr. Marlowe took notes. A few of them were from his family—his grandmother, his uncle and aunt in Washington, and his cousins in Connecticut—telling him how much they liked seeing him on *The Today Show*.

But the Marlowes couldn't believe all the producers who called to book Peter for their shows as well:

- *Good Morning America*
- *The View*
- *The Daily Show with Jon Stewart*
- *The Oprah Show*
- *The Late Show with David Letterman*
- *Conan*
- *Dr. Phil*

And then there were all the others. He got messages from publishers who wanted to give him a book deal, agents who wanted to get him acting gigs, and headmasters and principals who wanted him to attend their private schools. There were also professionals who offered to help him: speech therapists, psychologists, psychiatrists, neurologists, hypnotists, and even a few wackos who just wanted to make money off of him. Even while the Marlowes were listening to all the messages, the phone continued to ring, and they had to just ignore it.

Peter was so excited by all this attention. "*For goodness' sake*," he said. "*Most sweet voices.*"

His dad was actually interested in some off the offers. "You're a star, Peter," he said, "and we should make the best of it." He started scribbling down figures, trying to figure out how much money they could actually make from all of these appearances and offers.

But Peter's mom disagreed. "This is all too much too fast," she said. "I know I'm overwhelmed, and we certainly don't want to overwhelm Peter."

Peter, upset with his dad for starting to make plans without his input, replied, "*Some have greatness thrust upon 'em.*" After some more discussion, they all agreed not to accept any offers until after the school performance.

At school the following Monday, we rehearsed all of our scenes from *The 30-Minute Shakespeare*. During the palmers scene, when Peter and I got to the kiss, we did the air kiss thing Ms. Hastings had suggested. Then Rachel, who was playing the Nurse, interrupted us right away, so I felt a little better knowing the real kiss on stage wouldn't last very long anyway. We were only two days away from the big show, and we felt good about our scenes.

Ms. Hastings had discussed costumes with the class early on, and we all decided to keep it simple. All the Montagues would wear red, and all the Capulets blue. The other kids would wear jeans and colored T-shirts, but I was going to wear a blue dress. After the wedding, I would add a red scarf around my neck to symbolize that Juliet had become a Montague.

On Tuesday, our class went to the auditorium for our first dress rehearsal. It wasn't actually a *dress* rehearsal, since we were in our regular clothes, but it was an official run-through on the stage with all of our props. A few kids who didn't have any lines had worked on some cool music for the play, and it sounded great finally added into the scenes. And Cindy and Barry had even created a slideshow with images of Shakespeare and Verona, Italy, where the play was supposed to be taking place. The slideshow would be projected on a screen before the show began.

On our first try, we went through the whole play with only a few interruptions. It was amazing! Just about everyone had memorized his or her lines, and it sounded like a real play for the first time. Peter and I even got through our scenes with that air kiss without any problem. When we got to the last line of the play, we all cheered and practiced our group bow. Ms. Hastings told us that we'd done a great job and she was proud of us. As the bell rang, she reminded us to bring in our costumes the next day for the big performance.

On the bus ride home that day, Peter texted me to ask if we should rehearse again after school. I turned to him and said, "I think we're OK. We should just wait until show time. *What's done is done.*" Peter laughed, and I realized I had just quoted Shakespeare without meaning to.

"*We are such stuff as dreams are made on,*" he said. "*I dedicate myself to your sweet pleasure.*" Then he gave me that same funny look he'd given me on *The Today Show* and said, "*I burn, I pine, I perish.*"

I looked away and mumbled that I had a lot of homework to do and would be too busy to rehearse.

That night, I couldn't stop thinking about what was going on between Peter and me. I really liked him a lot, and he obviously really liked me, but it was all so public that I was scared. If only we'd been able to tell each other how much we liked each other without an audience of five million people watching us on national television. And now our first kiss was going to be in front of the whole school!

As I lay in bed, I quietly recited my lines for the balcony scene. *The 30-Minute Shakespeare* book had edited it quite a bit, but some of the best lines were still in it:

> *O Romeo, Romeo! Wherefore art thou Romeo?*
> *Deny thy father and refuse thy name;*
> *Or, if thou wilt not, be but sworn my love,*
> *And I'll no longer be a Capulet.*
> *My bounty is as boundless as the sea,*
> *My love as deep; the more I give to thee,*
> *The more I have, for both are infinite.*

I was getting groggy, but I pictured Peter as I whispered the final lines:

> *Good night, good night! Parting is such sweet sorrow,*
> *That I shall say good night till it be morrow.*

CHAPTER SIXTEEN

"THE PLAY'S THE THING"

Peter looked excited when he got to the bus stop that morning. I made the mistake of asking him how he felt. He replied, *"From this day to the ending of the world, we shall be remember'd; we few, we happy few, we band of brothers."*

"And sisters," I reminded him.

"Give me thy hand: I am sorry," he said. As he said this he got down on one knee and reached out to me. I quickly moved away. It was bad enough we were going to have to kiss each other in front of the whole school, but I didn't want him getting romantic on the bus stop.

"It's OK," I said. "Let's wait until we get on stage to start our scene."

He looked a little hurt, but as the bus arrived, he said, *"The play's the thing."*

Ms. Hastings had arranged with the principal that we'd be excused from our morning classes to rehearse and get ready for our

Shakespeare Festival. She called it an "in-school field trip," and then told us that "in-school field trip" was an oxymoron. I liked when she taught us literary terms with real examples.

Peter and I headed straight to the auditorium from the bus, and a lot of the kids were already there. It was cool to see everyone in their "costumes"—red for the Montagues and blue for the Capulets. Peter actually had one of his Hawaiian shirts on over his red shirt but said he'd take it off for the performance. We all were wearing jeans, except for a few characters like the Friar and the Prince, and it was easy to tell who was on which side.

Once everyone got settled, we did a dry run of the play. There were only a few slip-ups like when Gregory dropped his Nerf sword during the opening scene, when the Nurse forgot one of her entrances, and when Romeo killed Paris in the last scene, Paris laughed when he hit the ground. The end of the play when Romeo and I meet in the tomb, he [SPOILER ALERT!] drinks the poison, and I stab myself with his dagger was really cool. The class got really quiet at that point, and before we knew it, we were all up practicing our final bows. We were ready.

Fourth period started at a quarter after ten, and the whole school filed into the auditorium. It was show time! We watched nervously from backstage as everyone took a seat and the slideshow ran on the big screen.

Max started everything off perfectly. He quoted the Prologue loudly and clearly. The fight between the Montague guys and the Capulet guys with their Nerf swords went off without any problems, and the kids in the audience laughed a lot. When it was time for my entrance during the ball scene, Max, who was playing Lord

Capulet, took my arm and out we walked onstage. Music played in the background, and he began to speak:

> *Welcome, gentlemen! ladies that have their toes Unplagued with corns will have a bout with you. Ah ha, my mistresses! which of you all Will now deny to dance? Come, musicians, play. A hall, a hall! give room! and foot it, girls.*

The audience actually got it and laughed at his joke! Then we all joined in and did the Elizabethan dance Ms. Hastings had taught us. That was fun, but then it was time for Peter and me to do our first scene together, the palmers scene.

We walked slowly toward each other and began our shared sonnet. I was practically shaking in my shoes knowing the big kiss was coming. Peter took my hand and said his opening line, "*If I profane with my unworthiest hand.*" We were really into it. "*Then move not, while my prayer's effect I take. Thus from my lips, by yours, my sin is purged.*" And then it happened. Peter held my face and gave me this huge kiss right on the lips. The kids in the auditorium gave out a big "wooo" that seemed to last forever. While we were waiting for the audience to finish howling so I could say my next line, Peter whispered to me, "How did you like that, Emma?"

The audience finally quieted. I continued the scene: "*Then have my lips the sin that they have took,*" we kissed again, the Nurse came in to interrupt us, and we exited the stage.

Backstage, Peter looked at me and said, "We were great, Emma. I think the audience loved it."

"Oh my gosh, Peter!" I said. "Listen to you."

"I really love this acting stuff. It's so cool to be on stage."

"Peter," I said, "listen to what you're saying."

"Oh, I'm sorry," he said. "I should have said something about you. I really loved the kiss. And I really do..."

"*Peter!*" I almost shouted. "You're not speaking Shakespeare anymore! Don't you get it? Are you OK?" But before he could answer, Ms. Hastings told us to get ready for our balcony scene. Peter looked startled and like he wanted to respond, but we had to get in place for our entrance.

The rest of the play went by quickly, and it was finally time for the last scene, our death scene. Peter entered the tomb, drank the "poison" (fruit punch), kissed me again, and said his last line, "*Thus with a kiss, I die.*" He fell right next to me.

I took the Nerf sword from him and said, "*O happy dagger! This is thy sheath; there rust, and let me die.*" With that, I pretended to stab myself in the stomach and fell next to him. The Montague and Capulet parents, along with the rest of the cast, came onstage and said a lot of things about making peace, and the lights went out. Peter and I stood up and took our bows to a lot of applause and yelling from the audience. Peter grabbed my hand, and when I looked at him, he looked really happy. As the clapping died down, he gave me a big hug and took his final bow.

After our performance, everyone was backstage hugging and talking excitedly. Ms. Hastings gave a short speech and let us know how well we'd done. But then the bell rang, and it was time to go off to our next class—the in-school field trip was over.

CHAPTER SEVENTEEN

"WHAT'S DONE IS DONE"

When I got home from school that day, part of me was upset about the long kiss that Peter had given me in front of the whole school, but the other part of me was so excited. On top of that, I felt kind of bad for him that his claim to fame was over. All of the TV appearances, magazine interviews, and book offers were voided at exactly the moment he kissed me. It was sort of like we were Cinderella and Prince Charming, except instead of something wonderful happening when he kissed me, something awful happened. He didn't turn into a frog or anything. He just turned into Peter. Or was that really something awful?

As I said before, I was starting to feel differently about him, and it was clear he was feeling the same way toward me. But he no longer needed me to be his "designated speaker," as his dad had referred to me, so I wondered if our relationship would change. Would he still like me? Maybe the real question was, would I still like him?

A few days earlier my mom had said something about how Peter and I were codependent. I still had no idea what that meant, so I decided to looked it up on Wikipedia. Here's what it said:

> Codependency or Codependence is a tendency to behave in overly passive or excessively caretaking ways that negatively impact one's relationships and quality of life. It also often involves putting one's needs at a lower priority than others while being excessively preoccupied with the needs of others. Codependency can occur in any type of relationship, including in families, at work, in friendships, and also in romantic, peer or community relationships. This behavior may be characterized by denial, low self-esteem, compliance, and/or control patterns.

So I started a mental checklist about my relationship with Peter:

- ✓ I was his caretaker.
- ✓ I was putting my needs at a lower priority than his.
- ✓ I was excessively preoccupied with his needs.
- ✓ We obviously had a relationship (though it wasn't clear if it was peer or romantic).
- ✓ I had somewhat low self-esteem and was being pretty compliant.

I had it all. The article went on to say all this was unhealthy but that there were steps to overcome it. So I started to wonder if maybe the only reason I liked Peter was because I felt he needed me and, in a sense, I needed him. Now that he no longer needed me, would he find a new girlfriend? Now that I no longer needed him, would I lose interest in him as a boyfriend?

I was suddenly so confused and depressed. I'd noticed that after the newspaper article and *The Today Show*, more and more cute girls had started to show an interest in Peter, girls who used to make fun of him when he was "normal." And they were the most popular ones like Julie, Zoe, and Antonia. But no one seemed particularly interested in me. Not any of those girls, not any of the cute guys, and not even our teachers. Peter was "That Shakespeare Kid," and I was the Invisible Girl. I hadn't worried about it before because I'd known Peter needed me around. But now he wouldn't need me anymore.

I couldn't wait for my mom to get home so I could tell her what had happened during our performance and how I felt. I knew she'd have the right answer. She always did, even though I hated to admit it sometimes. I thought about calling her at work, but I knew I'd start crying and she'd only get upset. I got myself a glass of milk and opened up a box of Oreos—that always helped when I was sad.

Then the doorbell rang. I couldn't believe it when I looked out the window and saw Peter standing there. I opened the door and was almost surprised to hear him say something that wasn't from Shakespeare. "Hey Emma," he said. "I have something to tell you."

"Oh, good, Peter." I responded, feeling a little nervous. "I wanted to talk to you, too." I let him in, and we stood in the foyer.

"Me first," he said, excitedly. "I want to tell you how lucky I feel today."

"Lucky? But your whole Shakespeare career is over."

"I don't care about that."

"But what about all the TV shows and the magazines and all the rest of the stuff that was going to happen? You were so excited about all that. And your dad was hoping you'd make enough money for your college fund."

"Emma, you don't get it. What matters to me is I finally got my real voice back, and I can tell you in my own words how much I like you."

I was in shock. I couldn't believe he was choosing me over fame and money. "But you were going to be famous," I argued. "Everyone was going to..."

He cut me off. "Listen, Emma! It was sort of fun while it lasted, but it was pretty hard not being able to use my own words. Actually, in a lot of ways I hated it."

"You did? You seemed to be having such a good time."

"I know, I know. I acted like I was having a ball, but deep down I was miserable. Shakespeare did have a beautiful way of saying things, but I felt like I was being a phony most of the time. It was only when I was texting with you that I felt happy. I don't know what I would've done without you. I totally depended on you."

So I was right. We had just been codependent. "Did you say 'depended'? So, you just thought of me as someone you could depend on? Is that it?" I could feel my face starting to get red.

"What are you talking about? Why are you getting so angry?" Peter asked, looking confused.

"Because what we had was just a case of codependency. You depended on me, and I guess I depended on you. You needed me to translate for you, and in a way, I needed you so I could feel like I was a part of everything. But that's it. We can go back to being just two kids who live down the street from each other now." I couldn't hold back the tears anymore. They started streaming down my face.

"Where did you get all that psychology stuff? What are you talking about?"

"Actually, my mom mentioned it, and I looked it up on Wikipedia. It said it's an unhealthy relationship." I was really crying at that point.

"Will you stop? What do I have to say to you to make you believe I care for you? How about that I would trade everything that happened to me—everything, including the article in *Newsday*, *The Today Show* appearance, the YouTube videos, and all that attention—just to have been able to say 'I love you'?"

"You would have? Seriously?" I asked, smiling and sniffling through my tears.

"Absolutely seriously!" he said, grinning. "I love you!" At that, he pulled me toward him, looked me right in the eye, and gave me a huge kiss. It must have lasted a full minute and was so much better than the one we'd shared on stage. But suddenly we heard my mom's car pull into the driveway, and we sat down at the kitchen table, ate some Oreos, and had an actual conversation—without any mention of Shakespeare at all.

"BID ME FAREWELL"

I t's been about three months since all this happened. Summer came, and that meant the end of middle school. And yes, Peter and I are still going out. I have a job working as a "counselor in training" at a day camp, and Peter goes into New York City with his mom nearly every day to help out in her office. But when we do get together it's pretty special. I think that's all I'll say about that.

One of the things we've started doing together (and now you're sure that we're the biggest nerds in the world) is watch Shakespeare movies. Some of them are really good renditions. We really liked the version of *A Midsummer Night's Dream* with Kevin Kline in it. We also watched *Hamlet 2000* with Ethan Hawke and *Macbeth* with Patrick Stewart. But our favorite play is *Much Ado About Nothing*, and we love watching movie versions of it. We argue a lot about which version is better. My favorite is the 1993 version with Kenneth Branagh and Emma Thompson, but Peter prefers the 2013 one directed by Joss Whedon, starring Amy Acker and Alexis

Denisof. (You might remember them from that vampire TV series, *Angel.*)

We also watched a bunch of Shakespeare movie adaptations that don't even use Shakespeare language at all. So we've seen *She's The Man* based on *Twelfth Night; 10 Things I Hate About You*, which is a modern version of *The Taming of the Shrew;* and yes, we even watched *Gnomeo and Juliet.* They were all fun, but we both agree we like the real Shakespeare better.

It's almost September now, and soon it'll be time to start ninth grade. I'm really looking forward to high school. I heard the ninth grade kids get to read *A Midsummer Night's Dream,* and I really hope we get to act it out.

My guess is most kids have already forgotten about Peter's being "That Shakespeare Kid" and everything that happened to us, but that's OK.

I don't know how long Peter and I will remain boyfriend and girlfriend, but no matter what I'll always remember that amazing time I had with "That Shakespeare Kid."

The End

ADDENDUM

"SPEAK BUT ONE RHYME, AND I AM SATISFIED"

N ow that you've finished reading this book, it's your turn to take Mercutio's advice to Romeo in Act 2 and speak but one line of Shakespeare. So look through these lines and say just one out loud. And once you've done that, speak another and another and another. Yes, Peter has been cured of his condition, but he's certainly not cured of loving Shakespeare; nor is Emma, as we learn in the Epilogue. And although you've gotten through this book, I'll bet you're not through with Shakespeare, either.

[Shakespeare's lines quoted in this book were taken from all thirty-seven plays he wrote, as well as one of his sonnets.]

Chapter One: "*Come What May*"

O sleep! O gentle sleep.
Henry IV, Part 2 3.1

Good morrow, father.
Romeo and Juliet 2.3

Yes, better, sir.
Romeo and Juliet 1.1

But soft! What light through yonder window breaks?
Romeo and Juliet 2.2

Fair thoughts and happy hours attend on you.
The Merchant of Venice 3.4

How like a dream is this I see and hear.
The Two Gentlemen of Verona 5.4

It is a wise father that knows his own child.
The Merchant of Venice 2.2

Half sleep, half waking: but as yet, I swear, I cannot truly say how
I came here.
A Midsummer Night's Dream 4.1

What the dickens.
The Merry Wives of Windsor 3.2

Come what may.
Twelfth Night 2.1

Now, what news on the Rialto?
The Merchant of Venice 3.1

All the world's a stage, and all the men and woman merely players.
As You Like It 2.7

What's done cannot be undone.
Macbeth 5.1

'twas a rough night.
Macbeth 2.3

All shall be well.
A Midsummer Night's Dream 3.2

I thank you. I am not a man of many words, but I thank you.
Much Ado About Nothing 1.1

Parting is such sweet sorrow.
Romeo and Juliet 2.2

Chapter Two: "*I Will Wear My Heart upon My Sleeve*"

A horse! A horse! My kingdom for a horse!
Richard III 5.4

I will wear my heart upon my sleeve.
Othello 1.1

O brave new world that has such people in't.
The Tempest 5.1

Chapter Three: *"To Sleep: Perchance to Dream"*

For this relief, much thanks.
Hamlet 1.1

Alack, what noise is this?
Hamlet 4.5

I am ill at these numbers.
Hamlet 2.2

Madam, I am not well.
Romeo and Juliet 3.5

To sleep: perchance to dream: ay, there's the rub.
Hamlet 3.1

Chapter Four: *"So Bethumped with Words"*

Methinks I see these things with parted eye.
A Midsummer Night's Dream 4.1

But soft, methinks I scent the morning air.
Hamlet 1.5

All the world is cheered by the sun.
Richard III 1.2

Go Rot!
The Winter's Tale 1.2

I never was so bethumped with words.
King John 2.2

'Tis my occupation to be plain.
King Lear 2.2

Shall we go draw our numbers and set on?
Henry IV Part 2 1.3

To be or not to be? That is the question.
Hamlet 3.1

I am not merry.
Othello 2.1

Why, 'tis good to be sad and say nothing.
As You Like It 4.1

In sooth, I know not why I am so sad.
Twelfth Night 1.1

I have this while with leaden thoughts been pressed.
Othello 3.4

Say, why is this? Wherefore? What should we do?
Hamlet 1.4

Zounds!
Titus Andronicus 4.2

I am fortune's fool!
Romeo and Juliet 3.1

I thank you for your honest care.
All's Well That Ends Well 1.3

Good day and happiness.
As You Like It 4.1

The readiness is all.
Hamlet 5.2

To conclude, the victory fell on us!
Macbeth 1.2

Chapter Five: *"The Game Is Afoot!"*

Doubt thou the stars are fire; doubt that the sun doth move; doubt truth to be a liar; but never doubt I love.
Hamlet 2.2

Good night, good night! parting is such sweet sorrow, that I shall say good night till it be morrow.
Romeo and Juliet 2.2

The train approacheth.
Henry VI, Part 1 5.4

That book in many's eyes doth share the glory.
Romeo and Juliet 1.3

I can no other answer make but thanks.
Twelfth Night 3.3

Methinks nobody should be sad but I.
King John 4.1

They that pitch will be defiled.
Much Ado About Nothing 3.3

A foregone conclusion.
Othello 3.3

Strike upon the bell!
Macbeth 2.1

Lord, what fools these mortals be.
A Midsummer Night's Dream 3.2

O, I die for food!
As You Like It 2.6

The game is afoot!
Henry IV, Part 1, 1.3

A hit! A hit! A very palpable hit.
Hamlet 2.2

Hence! Home...get you home.
Julius Caesar 1.1

I shall catch the fly.
Henry V 5.2

I'll catch it ere it come to ground.
Macbeth 3.5

O, 'tis fair!
Troilus and Cressida 5.3

Fair is foul, and foul is fair!
Macbeth 1.1

What, up and down, carved like an apple.
The Taming of the Shrew 4.3

Alack!
Love's Labor's Lost 4.3

Full of sound and fury.
Macbeth 5.5

He comes the third time home.
Coriolanus 2.1

Have all his ventures failed? What, not one hit?
The Merchant of Venice 3.2

Now you strike like the blind man.
Much Ado About Nothing 2.1

He hath a lean and hungry look.
Julius Caesar 1.2

Taste your legs, sir; put them in motion.
Twelfth Night 3.2

You may go walk.
The Taming of the Shrew 3.1

Where shall I find one that can steal well?
Henry IV, Part 1 3.3

You have scarce time to steal.
Henry VIII 3.2

Stinking pitch.
The Tempest 1.2

As swift in motion as a ball.
Romeo and Juliet 2.5

That one error fills him with faults.
The Two Gentlemen of Verona 5.4

O hateful error.
Julius Caesar 5.3

The fool slides.
Troilus and Cressida 3.3

This was the most unkindest cut of all.
Julius Caesar 3.2

Ay, that way goes the game.
A Midsummer Night's Dream 3.2

What's done is done.
Macbeth 3.2

Chapter Six: *Parting Is Such Sweet Sorrow*

Good night, good night! Parting is such sweet sorrow, that I shall say good night till it be morrow.
Romeo and Juliet 2.2

Chapter Seven: *O, I Am Slain!*

Prithee, speak, how many score of miles may we well ride 'twixt hour and hour?
Cymbeline 3.2

There is much matter to be heard and learn'd.
As You Like It 5.4

Mine eyes smell onions; I shall weep anon.
All's Well That Ends Well 5.3

O wonderful, wonderful, and most wonderful! and yet again wonderful.
As You Like It 3.2

O, I am slain!
King Lear 3.7

She should have died hereafter.
Macbeth 5.5

Yes, yes; the lines are very quaintly writ.
The Two Gentlemen of Verona 2.1

Shall this our lofty scene be acted over?
Julius Caesar 3.1

Let me be your servant: though I look old, yet I am strong and lusty.
As You Like It 2.3

Get thee to a nunnery.
Hamlet 3.1

I prithee, take thy fingers from my throat.
Hamlet 5.1

My soul is too much charged with blood of thine already.
Macbeth 5.8

Do not you love me?
Much Ado About Nothing 5.4

Get you gone, you minimus.
A Midsummer Night's Dream 3.2

I do believe that these applauses are for some new honors.
Julius Caesar 1.2

Madam, good even to your ladyship.
The Two Gentlemen of Verona 4.2

Things that, to hear them told, have made me tremble; I will do it without fear or doubt.
Romeo and Juliet 4.1

Farewell! God knows when we shall meet again.
Romeo and Juliet 4.3

Chapter Eight: *"Full of Scorpions Is My Mind"*

Good morrow, gentle lady.
The Two Gentlemen of Verona 4.3

Full of scorpions is my mind.
Macbeth 3.2

Is there no way to cure this? No new device to beat this from my brains?
Henry VIII 3.2

Did you ever cure any so?
As You Like It 3.2

'Til then, adieu.
Romeo and Juliet 4.1

Chapter Nine: *"In My Head and in My Heart"*

I'll write it straight.
As You Like It 3.5

The matter's in my head and in my heart.
As You Like It 3.5

For my part, I care not.
Henry V 2.1

That shall be as it may.
Henry V 2.1

I dare not fight; but I will wink and hold out mine iron.
Henry V 2.1

Zounds, I would make him eat a piece of my sword.
Henry IV, Part 1 5.4

Then have at you with my wit! I will dry-beat you with an iron wit, and put up my iron dagger.
Romeo and Juliet 4.5

What would you have me do?
All's Well That Ends Well 5.2

Chapter Ten: *"The Traffic of Our Stage"*

Our revels now are ended. These our actors, as I foretold you, were all spirits and are melted into air, into thin air.
The Tempest 4.1

You are right, courteous knights.
Pericles 2.3

Chapter Eleven: *"Two Blushing Pilgrims"*

I'll perform it to the last article.
Othello 3.3

We must needs dine together.
Timon of Athens 1.1

A hundred thousand welcomes!
Coriolanus 2.1

Sit down and welcome to our table.
As You Like It 2.7

Chapter Twelve: *" 'Tis True: There's Magic in the Web"*

Sir, understand you this of me in sooth.
The Taming of the Shrew 1.2

Verily, I do not jest with you.
Coriolanus 1.3

Here I am to speak what I do know.
Julius Caesar 3.2

I have neither wit, nor words to stir men's blood: I only speak right on.
Julius Caesar 3.2

Thanks to all at once and to each one.
Macbeth 5.8

Friends, Romans, countrymen, lend me your ears;
I come to bury Caesar, not to praise him.
The evil that men do lives after them;
The good is oft interred with their bones.
Julius Caesar 3.2

Brutus was an honorable man.
Julius Caesar 3.2

Once more unto the breach.
Henry V 3.1

Chapter Thirteen: *"I Do Not Jest"*

Peace, you mumbling fool!
Romeo and Juliet 3.5

Ay, Madam, 'Tis in my memory lock'd.
Hamlet 1.3

Shall I compare thee to a summer's day?
Thou art more lovely and more temperate:
Rough winds do shake the darling buds of May,
And summer's lease hath all too short a date:
Sometime too hot the eye of heaven shines,
And often is his gold complexion dimm'd;
And every fair from fair sometime declines,
By chance or nature's changing course untrimm'd;
But thy eternal summer shall not fade
Nor lose possession of that fair thou owest;
Nor shall Death brag thou wander'st in his shade,
When in eternal lines to time thou growest:
So long as men can breathe or eyes can see,
So long lives this and this gives life to thee.
Sonnet 18

Yes, without all doubt.
Henry VIII 4.1

Am I so round with you as you with me, that like a football you do
spurn me thus?
The Comedy of Errors 2.1

The cat will mew and dog will have his day.
Hamlet 5.1

A horse! A horse! My kingdom for a horse!
Richard III 5.4

Faith, as you say, there's small choice in rotten apples.
The Taming of the Shrew 1.1

Give not this rotten orange to your friend.
Much Ado About Nothing 4.1

I have words to speak in thine ear will make thee dumb.
Hamlet 4.6

I am bound to you, that you on my behalf would pluck a flower.
Henry VI, Part 1 2.4

Teeth hadst thou in thy head when thou wast born, to signify thou camest to bite the world.
Henry VI, Part 3 5.6

The strawberry grows underneath the nettle and wholesome berries thrive and ripen best neighbour'd by fruit of baser quality.
Henry V 1.1

Pray you once more, is not your father grown incapable of reasonable affairs? Is he not stupid?
The Winter's Tale 4.4

You have dancing shoes with nimble soles.
Romeo and Juliet 1.4

His breath stinks with eating toasted cheese.
Henry VI, Part 2 4.7

Tis a lucky day, boy, and we'll do good deeds on it.
The Winter's Tale 3.3

If music be the food of love, play on.
Twelfth Night 1.1

The naked truth of it is, I have no shirt.
Love's Labor's Lost 5.2

Away! You are an ass, you are an ass.
Much Ado About Nothing 4.2

Pray, be not sick, for you must be our housewife.
Cymbeline 4.2

At Christmas I no more desire a rose than wish a snow in May's new-fangled mirth.
Love's Labor's Lost 1.1

Go, girl, seek happy nights to happy days.
Romeo and Juliet 1.3

She was a vixen when she went to school; and though she be but little, she is fierce.
A Midsummer Night's Dream 3.2

I have no words: My voice is in my sword: thou bloodier villain than terms can give thee out!
Macbeth 5.8

No words, no words: hush.
King Lear 3.4

Pray you, let's have no words of this.
Hamlet 4.5

Chapter Fourteen: *"Perchance You Wonder at This Show"*

But, soft! What day is this?
Romeo and Juliet 3.4

Good day at once.
Timon of Athens 3.4

A glooming peace this morning with it brings.
Romeo and Juliet 5.3

I have a faint cold fear thrills through my veins.
Romeo and Juliet 4.3

Fear comes upon me: O, much I fear some ill unlucky thing.
Romeo and Juliet 5.3

I have not slept one wink.
Cymbeline 3.4

I would give all my fame for a pot of ale and safety.
Henry V 3.2

By'r lady, he is a good musician.
Henry IV, Part 1 3.1

Ay, forsooth.
Romeo and Juliet 4.2

Fair thoughts and happy hours attend on you!
The Merchant of Venice 3.4

Frailty, thy name is woman.
Hamlet 1.2

Well enough, he said. God has given you one face, and you make
yourselves another.
Hamlet 3.1

Good morrow, noble sir.
Macbeth 2.3

Ay tis true: 'tis true 'tis pity; and pity 'tis 'tis true.
Hamlet 2.2

Farewell, good fellow.
Romeo and Juliet 5.3

I'll talk with you more anon.
All's Well That Ends Well 1.3

Farewell, dear father.
Romeo and Juliet 4.1

Adieu, my mother.
Richard II 1.3

Well, that fault may be mended with a breakfast.
The Two Gentlemen of Verona 3.1

They are never curst but when they are hungry.
The Winter's Tale 3.3

Let me shake thy hand.
Antony and Cleopatra 2.6

His very genius hath taken the infection of the device, man.
Twelfth Night 3.4

Be not afraid of greatness: some are born great, some achieve greatness and some have greatness thrust upon them.
Twelfth Night 2.5

Fair thoughts and happy hours attend on you.
The Merchant of Venice 3.4

Methought 'tis very strange. I have had a dream, past the wit of man to say what dream it was.
A Midsummer Night's Dream 4.1

O, I am mock'd...to make the world to laugh at me.
Pericles 5.1

Though this be madness, yet there is method in't.
Hamlet 2.2

Pardon, good father! good my mother, pardon!
The Merry Wives of Windsor 5.5

Perchance you wonder at this show.
A Midsummer Night's Dream 5.1

The time is out of joint.
Hamlet 1.5

Nay...It was Greek to me.
Julius Caesar 1.2

Thou know'st that we two went to school together.
Julius Caesar 5.5

Never was a story of more woe, then this of Juliet and her Romeo.
Romeo and Juliet 5.3

What's in a name? That which we call a rose by any other word would smell as sweet.
Romeo and Juliet 2.2

If music be the food of love, play on.
Twelfth Night 1.1

Who's there?
Hamlet 1.1

When shall we three meet again?
Macbeth 1.1

Now is the winter of our discontent made glorious summer by this sun of York.
Richard III 1.1

Plainly conceive, I love you.
Measure for Measure 2.4

Fare thee well.
Henry IV, Part 2 2.4

Prithee, who's there, besides foul weather?
King Lear 3.1

Chapter Fifteen: *"For Goodness' Sake"*
For goodness' sake.
Henry VIII 1.1

Most sweet voices.
Coriolanus 2.3

Some have greatness thrust upon 'em.
Twelfth Night 2.5

What's done is done.
Macbeth 3.2

We are such stuff as dreams are made on.
The Tempest 4.1

I dedicate myself to your sweet pleasure.
Cymbeline 1.6

I burn, I pine, I perish.
The Taming of the Shrew 1.1

O Romeo, Romeo! Wherefore art thou Romeo?
Deny thy father and refuse thy name;
Or, if thou wilt not, be but sworn my love,
And I'll no longer be a Capulet.
My bounty is as boundless as the sea,
My love as deep; the more I give to thee,
The more I have, for both are infinite.
Good night, good night! Parting is such sweet sorrow,
That I shall say good night till it be morrow.
Romeo and Juliet 2.2

Chapter Sixteen: *"The Play's the Thing"*

From this day to the ending of the world, we shall be remember'd;
we few, we happy few, we band of brothers.
Henry V 4.3

Give me thy hand: I am sorry.
The Tempest 3.2

The play's the thing.
Hamlet 2.2

Welcome, gentlemen! ladies that have their toes
Unplagued with corns will have a bout with you.
Ah ha, my mistresses! which of you all
Will now deny to dance? Come, musicians, play.
A hall, a hall! give room! and foot it, girls.
Romeo and Juliet 1.5

If I profane with my unworthiest hand.
Romeo and Juliet 1.5

Then move not, while my prayer's effect I take.
Thus from my lips, by yours, my sin is purged.
Romeo and Juliet 1.5

Thus with a kiss, I die.
Romeo and Juliet 5.3

O happy dagger! This is thy sheath; there rust, and let me die.
Romeo and Juliet 5.3

Made in United States
North Haven, CT
03 December 2021

11945657R00098